THE SMOKING BUN

CHELSEA THOMAS

1

A HAIRY SITUATION

*S*omething was wrong with Teeny.

Miss May and I were seated comfortably in our booth at Teeny's restaurant, *Grandma's*, but we could hear her slamming plates and grunting in frustration all the way back in the kitchen.

I cringed. From the sound of it, Teeny was going to destroy the entire kitchen before the end of the morning rush.

Miss May wiggled in her seat. "That's the fourth angry noise Teeny has made since we sat down. I'm telling you, something's up with her."

I took a big bite of pancake and a glob of buttery syrup dribbled down my chin. "The food is good as ever." Another loud slam emanated from the kitchen. "But yeah, maybe Teeny is worked up about something."

Miss May craned her neck to get a look back toward the kitchen. "She hasn't even come out to say hi yet. Do you think one of us offended her in some way?"

"She sounded fine when we talked on the phone last night."

Miss May rubbed her chin. "True. Something must've happened overnight that upset her. Should we go back into the kitchen to talk to her?"

I chuckled. It wasn't often that my aunt, Miss May, seemed shaken up by a social situation. When my parents died, for instance, she'd adopted 13-year-old me, planned the funeral, mourned the death of her sister and brother-in-law, and still only missed one day of work.

And when my fiancé who-shall-not-be-named left me at the altar, it was Miss May who suggested I come back to work at the orchard in Pine Grove and welcomed me with open arms. She was generally unflappable. So, yeah. Her worry over Teeny's kitchen explosions was odd.

But Miss May and Teeny had been best friends since before the dinosaurs. (*Don't tell them I said that!*) When one of them was upset, the other one usually knew the reason. So I suppose I understood why Teeny's disgruntled attitude and lack of hospitality concerned Miss May.

"I'm sure it's nothing," I said. "Want a bite of pancake?"

"Do you have any syrup left?"

Grinning, I slid my little pitcher of real New York maple syrup across the table. Miss May looked both ways, lifted the pitcher to her lips and took a small, slow sip. "That's so good," she said. "People say Vermont has all the good syrup but they're wrong. We've got it good down here too. And why wouldn't we? We've got plenty of maple trees and the best water in the United States."

"This maple syrup obsession is a new thing for you," I said. "But I'm starting to feel like you're Popeye and the syrup is spinach."

Miss May chuckled. "If this syrup was spinach I wouldn't be so soft around my waistline. Or my thighs. Or my upper arms. OK, fine. All of me."

"Well, all I'm saying is, I'm glad to see it bring you some strength during this difficult separation between you and Teeny."

Miss May gave me a playful shove. "We're not separated. I just hope everything's OK with her."

Suddenly the front door to the restaurant chimed and in walked Detective Wayne Hudson, precisely the man we were there to meet. Miss May perked up and gave Wayne a little wave. "Over here."

Wayne headed toward us with a small smile and a nod of the head. In my mind, his journey from the front door to our booth in the back of the restaurant took an eternity.

As he walked, I flashed back to all the strange, sometimes awkward, sometimes beautiful moments Wayne and I had shared.

I'd first met Wayne about a month or so after moving to Pine Grove, maybe less. He had been the first detective on the scene when I'd discovered a dead body on Miss May's farm. His broad shoulders and blue-green eyes had stopped me in my tracks and OK, maybe made me drool a little bit.

Since that day, Wayne and I had always been in one another's orbit, sometimes romantically. We'd shared a slow dance under the moonlight on the orchard. And we'd had more than a couple electric encounters — even though sometimes those encounters ended with Wayne pointing out the food in my hair. Wayne had helped Miss May, Teeny and I solve quite a few murders, even though the Pine Grove Police Department at large hadn't been helpful.

The guy was handsome, quiet, and so, so tall — *so why wasn't I dating him?* Well, Wayne hadn't always respected my skills as a sleuth, and we'd had our share of disagreements. Plus, I was dating the eccentric and absurdly sweet Germany Turtle. Yes, Germany was living in Africa doing important scientific work with lions, but we were making the long distance thing work. Sort of...

"Chelsea! Chelsea." Miss May nudged me from across the table. "Slide over. Make room for Wayne."

I glanced up. Wayne stood above me, smirking. *How long had he been standing there? How long had I been contemplating our romantic entanglement? Was there drool on my face?*

I snapped to attention. "Sorry. I was daydreaming. About llamas. We should have llamas on the farm."

"No we shouldn't," said Miss May. "Llamas are high maintenance and they spit."

"Anyway, sorry." I slid over and gave the seat beside me a firm pat, like I was greeting a Great Dane. "Take a seat, champ. Park it right there."

Wayne sat right where I patted. "Thanks, champ."

Miss May leaned toward Wayne with a glint in her eye. "So. Tell us what you've learned about the foot."

"Wow, Miss May. You get straight to it, don't you? I was hoping I could order a cup of coffee first. Maybe a couple of eggs."

A high-pitched voice rang out from nearby. "I can do eggs. Fine. How do you want them cooked?" My eyes shifted to the toward the sound of the voice. There stood Teeny, arms crossed and blue eyes glaring.

"Teeny," said Miss May. "Hi." Miss May seemed desperate for conversation but Teeny was in angry business mode.

"Hi." Teeny turned back to Wayne. "Fried? Scrambled? Medium, soft, hard? And do you want bacon or sausage or what? Out with it already."

"Sausage, I guess. Can you do it a little burnt if possible?" Wayne squeaked out his special request with fear but I related... So much stuff in life is better just a little burnt.

"Sausage. Fine. What else, Prince? Do you want alkaline-free water? High alkaline water? Free trade, single bean, triple roasted backwards brewed coffee? A napkin made of Egyptian cotton?"

"What's the thread count on that napkin?" Wayne asked. He was trying to lighten the mood, but Teeny wasn't having it.

"You get a paper napkin like everybody else, Detective!"

The corners of Wayne's mouth fell. "I'm sorry. Are you mad at me?"

Miss May shot a questioning glance toward Teeny. "I think she's mad at me. But I don't know why."

Teeny scoffed. "I'm not mad at you. May, when I'm mad at you, I tell you. Right?"

"Then what's the matter?" Miss May asked.

"I don't want to talk about it." Teeny looked back toward Wayne. "Have you given them the update on that severed foot or should I come back for that later?"

"Nobody wants to waste any time before talking about this foot," said Wayne. "I feel used."

"Get over it," said Teeny. "You're a police officer and you have information about a severed foot that a dog dug up at my friend's farm. It just so happens that Miss May, Chelsea, and I are the best amateur detectives in town, no offense to the police department, so give us the information. We need to start piecing this thing together."

Wayne hung his head and mumbled something.

I leaned forward. "What was that?"

Wayne mumbled a few more words. I could make out "foot," and "farm," but that was it.

"Speak up," said Miss May.

Wayne met Miss May's eyes. "We've deduced that the

foot belonged to a male somewhere between the ages of 30 and 50, most likely."

I lowered my fork and looked up at Wayne. "I'm sorry. I'm confused. The police department has had that foot for at least a month. I thought you were bringing it to a lab or getting forensic evidence or something."

"No lab for feet. Not around here. It's not in our budget."

"So you and the other detectives have just been standing around looking at the foot?" Teeny asked. "'Looks like a foot to me, Bob. What do you think?' 'Yes. That's a foot. OK. Want to go to lunch?'"

Wayne bristled. "We got some information."

"We already had that information," said Miss May. "Of course the foot belonged to a male. There were visible hairs on the knuckles of the toes."

"Women can have hairy toe knuckles too," I said. "Not that I do. Not really. No one would say I have hairy toes. I just have some hairs on my toes. Sorry, what were you saying, Miss May?"

Miss May, Teeny, and Wayne all stared at me. I had a talent for sticking my slightly hairy foot into my mouth.

"I wasn't saying anything of note," said Miss May. "Just letting the detective know that the three of us needed mere moments to draw the same conclusion that it took the entire Pine Grove Police Department a month to figure out."

"To be fair, we were busy. Humphrey's dog ran away. We had to recover the canine."

"And I'm so glad they found Semolina so fast," Miss May said. "But I thought Humphrey found his dog over in the neighbor's yard eating tomatoes out of the greenhouse."

Wayne gulped. "That's true. But we did a lot of investigating prior to that. And Humphrey didn't tell us the dog had been found so we also did quite a bit of investigating after that."

"This is ridiculous," said Teeny.

"I'm sorry," said Wayne. "But rest assured, we're still looking for more clues about the severed foot and that body it was attached to. I'll keep you all updated, I promise."

Suddenly, Teeny's eyes widened and her mouth tightened in fury. She pointed over at the entrance to the restaurant. "Oh no. You are not welcome here. Get out of my restaurant."

I followed Teeny's gaze to an enormous, imposing man, hulking in the doorway. He was bald, with a hefty beard and a small gold earring in his left ear. A sleeve of tattoos poked out underneath the cuff of his flannel shirt.

I had no idea who that man was. But I had a sneaking suspicion he was somehow the cause of Teeny's murderous mood. And I wanted to find out why.

2

BUCKING BRONCO

"*I* will never serve you food in this restaurant," Teeny said. "You are a thief and a criminal. And I hate your earring and I hate your tattoos."

"I would never eat here, Teeny," the man grunted. "The only reason I came this morning was to tell you to stop leaving threatening voicemails on my phone."

I leaned toward Miss May. "Three questions... Who is this guy? What are they arguing about? And what do you think of the earring and the tattoos?"

Miss May whispered back. "His name is Buck. He's the new head chef at *Peter's Land and Sea*. I have no idea what they're arguing about. And I'm fine with the earring but I'd have to see more of the ink before forming an opinion."

"Aw, poor little Buck felt threatened by my voicemails," Teeny sneered. "Little boy got scared. Get over it. Thief."

Bucks laughed. "Chefs are inspired by one another's recipes all the time. I built on something you created. I made it better. That's not being a thief. That's called the creative process. Nothing new is left to make. *The Beatles* wrote all the good songs. Everyone else has just been rewriting them for 60 years."

"So you admit I'm as good as the Beatles." Teeny raised her eyebrows.

"Of course not. You're not even a real chef. If you were anything more than a glorified short-order cook, you'd understand the broader philosophical principles of creativity at play here. But how could I ever expect you to understand? You're just a diner girl who knows how to work the griddle."

"Joke's on you then, Bucky Boy. You stooped so low that you stole from a lowly diner girl!" Teeny wagged her finger at Buck. "You've got some nerve, talking about the creative process... Hashbrown lasagna is my signature dish. I had lines out the door for weeks! People waiting just to try it. City people, upstate people. The entirety of the tri-state area came to this restaurant to try my HBL. Now another restaurant in the same ZIP Code is serving it? That's preposterous. And it's illegal. It's not like *McDonald's* would allow you to open up a restaurant next door to them and sell a McChicken sandwich. Because that's stealing."

Buck held up his hand to silence Teeny in the most condescending way possible. "Like I said, I didn't steal your recipe. I built upon it. Your hashbrown lasagna is a little soggy, if you ask me. There's too much cheese. But that's to be expected at an establishment like this." Buck gestured around the cute and cozy restaurant like it was a rat-infested alleyway. "*At Peter's Land and Sea,* we like to take simple dishes and elevate them. That's why I've reimagined hashbrown lasagna with crispier potatoes, top-of-the-line cheese and, of course, truffle oil to top it all off. People have been raving. You should come by sometime. Taste it for yourself."

Teeny gritted her teeth. "You know what? Fine. I will try

it myself." Teeny gestured back to me and Miss May. "All three of us will come by. In fact, we'll go right now to taste your masterpiece. I'd love to look in Petey's eyes and ask him how he's allowing this treachery to go in under his roof. I trained that boy in this very restaurant."

Buck shrugged. "So your argument is with him."

Teeny dismissed Buck with a wave of her hand. "He's barely out of diapers. You're grown-up and ugly already. My argument is with you. Take me to that restaurant."

Buck took out his smart phone, opened an app and started scrolling. "Let me see here... Let me see..."

Teeny leaned forward like an angry, curious squirrel. "What are you doing? What is that? Are you stealing more recipes?"

"Of course not. I'm checking the app that my restaurant uses to handle reservations. That's how most nicer places handle bookings. Not a problem for a greasy spoon like this. But in fine dining, we can get booked up days, weeks, or even months ahead."

"I hate you," said Teeny.

"Me too," I said.

"So do I," said Miss May.

"Terrific. Glad to be hated. It looks like we have one table open—"

"Great. Let's go," said Teeny.

"Tomorrow morning. 7 AM."

"You're open that early?" asked Miss May.

Buck grinned. "City commuters stop in before the train if they want to have a gourmet breakfast."

Teeny slammed her palms on our table. "We'll be there."

3

A BRUNCH TO DIE FOR

*W*e arrived at *Peter's land and Sea* at promptly 6:45 AM. The early October air was crisp and refreshing. Hazy, early morning sun burned through an overcast sky. And, much to Teeny's disappointment, a line of well-dressed patrons had already formed out front.

A handsome young couple waited patiently, rocking a newborn in a stroller. A group of six friends, all somewhere in their twenties, took photos in front of the restaurant signage. An elderly man waited in a lawn chair, flipping through the pages of the most recent *New Yorker* magazine.

Teeny threw up her hands and brought them down with a resounding clap on her thighs. "Who are all these people? Not a single one of them is local, I'll tell you that. These are strangers invading our peaceful little town."

"You know how it works, Teeny," said Miss May. "When a restaurant in Pine Grove gets the right kind of buzz the city people flock up in droves."

"Well I only like it when they do that for my restaurant. Look at them in their pointy little shoes and their tiny little jeans. These people don't eat. They're too skinny to eat. They're just here to take pictures and make me mad."

Teeny charged up to the young couple as they continued to rock their baby in the stroller. "Excuse me. Who are you? Why are you here?"

The young mother blanched. "I'm sorry. Excuse me?"

Teeny adopted a firmer tone. "I said, who are you. Why are you in Pine Grove? Where are you from?"

The man stepped forward. "We're visiting Pine Grove from Astoria, Queens. We try a great new restaurant every Sunday for brunch. Our reservation isn't until eight, but we wanted to get here early." The man couldn't hide a giddy little smile. "We're so excited to try that truffle hashbrown lasagna."

Teeny gasped. "That's my hashbrown lasagna. I created it. Did you know that? The chef in there steals recipes from other local restaurants and passes them off as his own."

The man gave Teeny a quizzical look. "I'm pretty sure *Peter's Land and Sea* invented HBL."

The woman nodded. "Hashbrown lasagna was definitely invented here. I can't wait to try it! I heard that it's perfectly crunchy with not too much cheese. Too much cheese can ruin anything. You know?"

Teeny stopped her foot on the ground. "I know no such thing!"

Miss May put her hands on Teeny's shoulders and pulled Teeny back a few inches. "I'm sorry. You seem like a happy couple. Please excuse my friend. We haven't had our coffee yet. The truth is, the recipes here are stolen and it's an atrocity. But you two enjoy your meal. Your baby is adorable."

I looked down at the baby. She was chubby and red and

had the cutest little brown eyes. I swear she winked at me when I waved hello. "She really is so cute," I said.

The young couple beamed. "Thank you. Her name is Astrid. We just hope that one day she'll appreciate that we took her for such fine culinary experiences as an infant."

Miss May scratched her head. "Can Astrid already eat regular food?"

The man shook his head. "Not yet. But we're getting a head start on developing her pallet at a young age through scent and texture, mostly. She can already smell a truffle from a mile away."

"Like a pig," I said.

The couple looked at me, aghast.

"Sorry," I said. "It's just, pigs find truffles, so... You know what? Nevermind."

A woman in her thirties approached. She had her hair styled like a 1950's pinup girl and she wore a poodle skirt to match. Like Buck, her arms were covered in tattoos, and she had a perfect row of tiny little teeth, each one the exact same size. "Hi everyone. My name is Hannah and I'm the hostess here at *Peter's Land and Sea*. Welcome to the restaurant. Do you all have a reservation?"

We murmured the affirmative, as did the young couple and a few other groups around us.

"That's so terrific," Hannah said in a gentle tone. "And I couldn't help but notice there was a bit of a disagreement occurring over here." She gestured between Teeny and the young couple. "Is there a problem I can help with?"

"Sure. Tell Big Ugly Buck to stop stealing my recipes."

Hannah grimaced. "You must be Teeny. My husband told me you and your friends had a reservation this morning. More like he warned me, actually. I would say it's a pleasure to meet you but you just called my husband an ugly thief."

Teeny shook her head. "You married that tattooed moose? I want to hate you but now I feel bad for you."

Miss May snickered. "Teeny."

Teeny held up her hands in apology. "Alright. I'm sorry. Is our table almost ready?"

"That's actually why I came out here this morning. There's a bit of a backup in the dining room. All reservations will be delayed half an hour. We thank you in advance for your understanding."

A loud rumble emanated from my stomach in response to Hannah's news and I did my best to refrain from throwing my eyes to the heavens and screaming "Why? Why??? Why must my breakfast be delayed!?"

That may seem dramatic. But I was hungry, OK? And I needed to visit the little girl's room. "Can I use the bathroom while we wait?" I asked.

I took a step around Hannah, anticipating that she would be fine with me visiting the lavatory. But Hannah blocked my path. "I'm sorry. I'm afraid we're at capacity and I can't allow you to use the restroom. The fire marshal's been breathing down our neck for a week now. I suppose that's one of the downsides of enormous popularity."

"...but you're not open yet," I said.

"Ah, we have a private party. Very early risers."

"So you won't let my niece use the bathroom?" said Miss May. "That has to be illegal."

Hannah shrugged. "Feel free to head back into town to use the bathroom somewhere else. But I can't guarantee that your space will be available when you return."

"You know what, it's fine," I said. "Thanks for letting us know about the delay. Looking forward to trying the food."

Teeny glared after Hannah as Hannah walked away, then turned to me. "We can head into town to find a bathroom if you need it, Chelsea. My grudge against that tattooed monster can be put aside if you're about to pee your pants."

"Don't worry about it," I said. "I'm going to go around the back, sneak through the kitchen and use the employee bathroom."

Miss May grinned. "Spoken like a true sleuth. Don't get caught, OK?"

I scoffed. "Do I ever?"

4

TAKING OUT THE TRASH

S neaking into bathrooms in restaurants where I am not a customer has always been a hobby of mine. It's a skill that I developed during my time living in New York City. And I consider myself a master of the art.

Once, during my first year in Manhattan, I had to go to the bathroom while I was in the heart of Chinatown. There were no available public restrooms or coffee shops so I went to the nearest Chinese restaurant and told the hostess I was early for a meeting with a large group of friends.

The hostess sat me at a large, circular table in the middle of the upscale restaurant. She brought me water and a menu and began to take my order. I asked the waitress to give me a few minutes to think about what I wanted, all the while scheming to sneak to the bathroom at the first available moment. Then, when she turned her back, I scuttled to the bathroom with my head hung low. When I emerged from the lavatory the hostess was standing there, waiting for me. No words were necessary. I knew that she knew and she didn't look happy about it.

After a few seconds of uncomfortable eye contact, the

hostess stepped aside and gestured toward the door. I exited, cheeks flushed with both shame and pride. Yes, I'd lied my way into using the bathroom at a nice restaurant. That made me feel bad. But I no longer had to pee, thank goodness, and that made me feel good.

I shook off the memory of the Chinese restaurant as I approached the back entrance to *Peter's Land and Sea*. Glancing around to make sure no one was nearby, I hurried toward the kitchen entrance. But I stopped when I heard booming voices arguing inside.

I peeked into the kitchen. The voices belonged to Petey, Teeny's former employee and the current owner of the restaurant, and Buck, Teeny's mortal enemy.

Petey and Buck were walking right toward me. My eyes darted around the back area, looking for a hiding spot. I didn't have many options so I jumped into a dumpster and closed the lid just as Petey and Buck emerged from the restaurant. Lucky for me it was first thing in the morning so there wasn't much trash in the dumpster yet. I peeked out the crack in the lid and watched as Petey and Buck bickered.

"You work for me, Buck," Petey said. "You need to cook what I tell you to cook."

"Not a chance, kid. That there is my kitchen. And in my kitchen I don't take orders from anyone."

"I'm the owner of the restaurant."

"You knew my reputation when you hired me. I get results because I do everything the way I want. I'm a rockstar chef and that's all part of the package. I almost had a show on *Food Network*, you know."

"You talk about that show all the time," said Petey. "I don't care."

"It was going to be called *Buckingham's Palace: An Exploration of the Best Food the World Has to Offer*."

"But you lost the deal. Because you're mean and selfish and you won't take orders. Even from your boss, the owner of this restaurant. Me."

Buck paced back and forth. "No." He raised his voice. "I will not let some twerp little boy talk to me that way. You need me, kid. See that line of people? They're not here for you. When you were doing all the cooking, no one came to your sad establishment but the crusty old locals. And they only showed up out of sympathy. You're in over your head."

"I never said I don't need you," said Petey. "But we have to be a team."

"Disgusting. I hate when people say I have to be part of some kind of team. No. That's not the way kitchens work, man. You'd know that if you paid your dues like I did. It's a food chain in there. I'm at the top and everybody else is at the bottom."

"But I am the owner of the restaurant." Petey's voice squeaked when he got excited. "I am at the top of the food chain. By definition."

"That's where you're wrong, little boy. You want this restaurant to thrive, you're going to do things my way. And that's final." Buck shoved the door to the kitchen open and stormed inside.

Petey started to say something as Buck charged away, but his words soon morphed into a warbled soup of unintelligible vowels. I popped open the lid of the dumpster to get a better view. Petey sat on the curb, hung his head and sobbed.

"It's OK, Petey," I said.

Petey looked up with a start. "Chelsea. You're in the dumpster." He stood and helped me out. "You're lucky it's empty."

I smoothed my clothes and looked Petey square in the

eye. "You're right. That would've been horrific had the dumpster been full. I mean, it still wasn't fun, but it could've been way worse."

"You got that right. By the end of the day that thing smells like cigarettes and fish eyeballs."

I put my hand on Petey's shoulder. "Sorry I was eavesdropping. I didn't mean to. But uh, that seemed rough."

"He's out of control," said Petey.

"At least people are coming to the restaurant."

Petey nodded. "Wait. You never told me why you were in the dumpster."

"Oh yeah," I said. "Your wonderful hostess wouldn't let me inside to use the bathroom until our reservation was ready. So I snuck around back. But when I heard you and Buck--"

"Your detective instincts kicked in and you hid in the trash?"

"Yes. Detective instincts. That, and I'm generally afraid of conflict," I said.

Petey gestured toward the restaurant with his head. "Come on. I'll get you a table right away. No more waiting."

I followed Petey to the front of the restaurant. But my feet grew heavier with each step I took. I had the familiar bad feeling that something bad was brewing in Pine Grove. And, sooner rather than later, I was proven right.

5

HASHING IT OUT

*P*etey led us through his well appointed, upscale dining room to a four top table near the front windows. An old woman grumbled with discontent, noticing that we'd clearly cut the line, but Petey didn't seem to mind. In fact, there was a little smile on his face as he brushed past the woman. "Sorry, VIP," he said. "Teeny gave me my first job in the restaurant business."

"Save it, kid," Teeny grunted. "We're competitors now. And you're stealing my hashbrown lasagna."

"I think maybe we should blame the chef for that," I said. "Remember, earlier? You said we should blame the chef."

Teeny pouted. "Well I changed my mind. I blame everyone who works here." Teeny pointed at a pretty, doe-eyed waitress. "You know what you've done." She pointed at several other servers. "And you. And you. And you."

Petey pulled out a seat for Teeny and tried to change the subject. "Anything you order this morning will go straight to the front of the line. Just say the word and I'll have it out faster than a cook at *Grandma's*."

"So you think you're faster than me too." Teeny shook her head. "This generation doesn't appreciate anything."

Petey murmured an apology and hurried away, bumping into not one but three tables as he bustled toward the kitchen.

Petey's menu was unlike anything I'd seen in Pine Grove before. There was the truffle oil hashbrown lasagna, of course. But there were also breakfast tacos made with Kobe beef. And there were several dishes that featured exotic mushrooms, and another titled simply, "breakfast caviar."

Teeny slapped her menu down and took a big sip of her water. "This is absurd. Pine Grove needs a nice restaurant, sure. But this stuff is so snooty. And it doesn't even sound good. Nobody actually wants to eat this stuff. They just want to tell their friends that they've eaten this stuff."

Miss May chuckled. "Well said."

"I'm ordering hashbrown lasagna," said Teeny. "I need to see it with my own eyes."

A few moments passed, then a waiter showed up and the three of us ordered our food. Once the waiter had disappeared to punch in the order, I made sure the coast was clear, then I told Miss May and Teeny all about the argument I'd heard between Petey and Buck. Miss May and Teeny were the best audience anyone could hope for when telling a story. They nodded at all the right moments, they laughed when I said I was in the dumpster and they gasped whenever appropriate. *OK, Teeny even gasped a few times when it made no sense.*

When I was finally finished talking Miss May leaned back and shook her head. "I was wondering why you suddenly showed up with Petey and said our table was ready."

I nodded. "I suppose he felt weird after I saw him cry. He figured it was the least he could do."

"I can't believe the poor little tadpole was out there blubbering," said Teeny. "That settles it. I'm back on Petey's side. Buck is the bad guy here."

"Couldn't be more clear to me," I said.

Teeny rolled her eyes as a waitress approached with our food. Miss May had ordered the Kobe beef tacos. I'd gone with the unpronounceable mushroom omelette. And Teeny had ordered the hashbrown lasagna, as promised. Each dish was placed on the table with grace and its ingredients were announced one-by-one, which sent Teeny's eyes rolling so far back in her head I worried she'd never recover them.

"Enough already," said Teeny. "We're not British royalty. Just toss the food down and let us start eating."

"My apologies," said the waitress.

Teeny grabbed her fork and grimaced like she was about to eat live earthworms. "Alright. Let's dig into these abominations."

The hashbrown lasagna crunched under the weight of Teeny's fork. She gathered up a big bite and put it in her mouth. For a split-second it seemed as though Teeny might be enjoying the food. Then she discreetly spat the hashbrown lasagna back onto her fork and took another big sip of water.

"Not good?" asked Miss May.

"It's disgusting," said Teeny. "The truffle oil is overpowering. I can't eat that."

I wondered if Teeny really hated the food or if she was just being spiteful. So Miss May and I dug in too, trying Teeny's food and then our own. Teeny was right — the fancy ingredients were all overbearing and none of the food tasted like anything but its most expensive component. Between the three of us I'd be surprised if we swallowed one whole bite.

"Why are people lining up for this junk?" asked Teeny.

Miss May shrugged. "Sometimes if a place gets good reviews, people stop being able to tell for themselves whether or not it's good. Social bias. They hear from so many people that the food is delicious, they're afraid to disagree."

"I think all of Hollywood operates like that," I said. "Everyone is afraid to have their own taste."

Miss May pushed her plate away from her. "That explains why so many movies are bad."

I made a stop at the bathroom before we left, but a huge line had formed and I didn't want to wait. I vaguely remembered from when Petey had given us a grand opening tour that the restaurant had another bathroom upstairs, so I climbed the rickety old staircase near the front entrance to find out if my memory was correct.

The second floor of *Peter's Land and Sea* was a large banquet space that did not get much use. Sure enough, however, there was a bathroom along the far wall. I pushed the door open but it got stuck on something. I leaned into the door with my shoulder to try to push it open further, but the door wouldn't budge.

"Hello?" I called out. "Is someone in there?"

No one responded so I slithered through the opening in the doorway and stepped into the small bathroom.

For a moment I couldn't make any sense of the scene before me. There was a sink and a toilet, of course. But there was also a man sprawled across the floor in a terrible, unnatural position.

A pool of dark red fluid ran from the man's head and streaked through the white grout in the tiles. And a leaky faucet made a horrible dripping noise that made my hair stand on end.

I took a deep breath and made my way over to the man. I crouched down to get a look at his face. It was Buck, Petey's head chef. His skin was cold to the touch. And when I raised his hand and dropped it, the hand thudded to the floor, lifeless.

Buck was dead. And I had a feeling it would be up to me, Teeny, and Miss May to find out how he died and, probably, who killed him.

6

OVERDONE

*O*ver the course of the investigations I had
conducted with Teeny and Miss May, I had learned
that it's often best for us to survey the scene of the crime
before the police interfere. So I barricaded myself in the
bathroom with the dead body and texted Teeny and Miss
May to tell them to come upstairs. I tried not to look at
Buck's dead body as I waited, but morbid curiosity drew my
eyes to the corpse.

Based on the position of Buck's body, I deduced that he
had fallen to his death from a standing position and had
not, rather, been engaged in a struggle on the floor at the
time of his death.

I also noticed a crack on the tiled wall slightly above the
floor that had been spattered with blood. It appeared to me
that Buck might have hit his head on the tile when he had
fallen down.

Although Buck had been wearing his chef's whites
during his argument with Petey out by the dumpster, when
he died he was wearing a crisp black T-shirt. *That could
easily be explained*, I thought. Perhaps the chef's whites were

uncomfortable or had gotten dirty, so Buck had taken them off to come up to the bathroom.

There was a soft knock at the bathroom door and I stood up right. "Hello?"

"Chelsea. Let us in."

I held open the bathroom door and Miss May and Teeny squeezed their way inside just as I had. When Teeny saw the dead body she widened her eyes and clasped her hands over her mouth. "Oh my goodness... Chelsea... Did you..."

"I didn't kill Buck," I said. "I can't believe you think I'm capable of that."

Teeny stammered for a few seconds but couldn't find words, so she gave me an apologetic shrug instead.

Miss May crouched beside the body to get a closer look. I took the opportunity to fill Teeny and Miss May in on the details I had observed. Teeny couldn't look away from the body, and as I spoke the horrified expression on her face didn't fade. But Miss May paid careful attention to my words and nodded at the important details.

When I stopped talking, Miss May pointed over to the trashcan beneath the sink. "You missed an important piece of information."

I peered into the garbage. A plump, sugary cinnamon bun, the edges burnt and charred, sat at the top of the trashcan with one bite taken out. "I'm confused. That's a cinnamon bun."

Teeny looked over. "I bet they stole my recipe for that, too."

Miss May shot Teeny a look. "Everyone knows I make the best cinnamon buns in town."

"Whatever," said Teeny.

"How is this cinnamon bun related?" I asked. "I mean,

it's slightly burnt, so I'm surprised anyone took a bite of it, but—"

"Touch it," said Miss May. "I suspect it's still warm."

I looked down at the cinnamon bun like it was the monster under my bed. "I don't want to touch that."

Miss May's stern glanced insisted. I steeled my nerves by shaking out my hands then I reached out and touched the cinnamon bun. "You're right. It's still warm. What does that mean?"

"It means I don't think Buck died from this head wound. The gash isn't very deep and it doesn't appear that there's a deadly amount of blood here."

"You think someone poisoned that cinnamon bun," said Teeny. "I knew it. That's what I was thinking. Poisoned baked goods are such a tragic way to die. Cinnamon buns should be a force for good in this world. Never evil." Teeny glanced over at Buck who remained prone on the floor. "Poor guy thought he was sneaking up to the bathroom to eat a sweet treat in secret. Then this happens."

I spotted something across the room. "I think I found another clue. Look at the toilet."

I stood above the toilet. Teeny and Miss May crowded around me, stepping over Bucks corpse to get as close as possible. "I don't know how I missed this the first time. But it's clear this doesn't add up."

"What?" Teeny threw up her hands in impatient frustration.

"Hold on," said Miss May. "I want to figure this out."

Miss May leaned over and looked in the toilet bowl. Nothing but a little bit of clear water. She craned her neck to the right and to the left to look around the sides of the bowl. Everything appeared normal there as well. My chest swelled with pride as Miss May scratched her head, looking stumped. It wasn't often that I discovered an important clue before Miss May, so I allowed myself to gloat for a few seconds.

"Want me to tell you what the great Chelsea sees?" I asked.

Miss May closed her eyes and nodded. "Please, oh Great One. Enlighten me."

"This toilet is running. And the water is low. I think this bathroom is out of order." I tried to flush the toilet and the loose handle jiggled and clanked. Sure enough, the bowl was not functioning.

"Now this is a conspiracy," said Teeny. "Buck came up to a nonworking bathroom... With a cinnamon bun? Maybe it's how I said. Maybe he was just eating in secret."

"But who chooses to eat in a bathroom?" Miss May asked.

"Exactly," I agreed. "And who chooses to go to a bathroom that's not functioning if they need to relieve themselves?"

We all stood there in silent thought. I looked down at Buck, then I felt disrespectful so I looked away. Then I focused my eyes back on the bowl. After a few seconds of listening to the perpetually running toilet, I looked over at Teeny and Miss May. They looked just as confused as I felt.

"I feel bad," said Teeny. "Real bad."

Miss May nodded. "It's always sad to find a dead body."

"This one's even worse for me," said Teeny. "I called this guy ugly to his face right before he died. I said a lot of nasty stuff to him."

"That's OK, Teeny," I said. "Buck was kind of a nasty guy, all due respect. You should have heard him yelling at Petey. And he stole your recipe. And—"

There was a knock at the door. Miss May, Teeny and I

stood perfectly still like we had been caught robbing a bank. Miss May cleared her throat. "Yes?"

Suddenly the door edged open and a young woman stepped through. I recognized her as one of the waitresses from the restaurant, Rebecca. When Rebecca saw Buck's dead body, she screamed and backed against the wall.

We had no choice but to call the cops.

7

COP OUTS

*P*ine Grove is one of those unfortunate towns to have a prideful, arrogant chief of police. Chief Sunshine Flanagan had risen through the ranks quickly, which I think contributed to her unpalatable personality and her insecurity. It was never fun when she arrived on the scene of a crime.

Aside from her gruff and disrespectful personality, Sunshine also had a preternatural ability to make me feel like an ugly duckling. Her legs were taller than my whole body, and her flowing red hair was always wavy and shiny.

That morning, Sunshine insisted on splitting me, Teeny, and Miss May apart so she could "compare our stories." She wouldn't let any other detectives speak to us, especially Wayne. Sure, maybe Wayne had a slight bias in our favor. But I was also pretty sure that Sunshine had her lady heart set on Wayne and she resented his affection for me.

It was at least three hours before the three of us were released from police custody. And once we were together again, we all agreed: it was time for lunch.

Half an hour later, Miss May and I were seated in our

favorite booth at Teeny's restaurant, ready to eat. Although we had told Teeny that we'd be fine with something simple, Teeny was determined to "cook us something nice." And she insisted we wait to discuss the case until the food was ready. So Miss May and I sat in pained silence for what felt like eternity as Teeny cooked.

My eyes drooped as we waited and my forehead was about to hit the table when Teeny finally appeared and placed a large platter of macaroni and cheese on the table. Somehow I felt more awake as soon as I saw the food. "Macaroni and cheese. Yum."

I grabbed a fork but Teeny held up her hand to stop me from taking a bite. "No, no. This isn't a regular old macaroni and cheese. It's truffle macaroni and cheese."

Miss May narrowed her eyes. "Where did you get truffles?"

"I swiped a few during all the commotion at *Peter's Land and Sea*," said Teeny. "No one was looking, they were all too concerned with the murder or whatever."

Miss May hung her head. "It won't be good for our credibility as sleuths if we steal from crime scenes."

"They stole from me first," said Teeny. "Take a bite, let me know what you think." Miss May glared. Teeny huffed impatiently. "I won't do it again, OK? Now take a bite. You're ticking me off!"

Miss May and I each took a bite of the macaroni and cheese. I cocked my head to the side and looked at Teeny. I couldn't taste anything other than cheese and pasta, which was how I liked it. "This has truffles in it?"

"Shoot. You can't taste them." Teeny shook her head. "They say a little goes a long way so I only used a tiny bit."

I giggled. "Fine with me. I'm a purist, anyway. When it comes to mac and cheese, at least."

"Take a seat, Teeny," Miss May said. "Let's talk about this murder."

Teeny slid into the booth and devoured a heaping forkful of macaroni and cheese. "Are we sure it's a murder?" Teeny asked. "I know the scene suggested murder and usually, in Pine Grove, it is murder... But I was recently watching Season 9, Episode 28 of *Jenna and Mr. Flowers*—"

"Real life is not like the BBC," Miss May said. "You need to stop comparing our cases to your favorite shows!"

"Will you let me talk?" asked Teeny.

Miss May gestured for Teeny to continue and Teeny got right back into her story. "OK. So. In this episode of *Jenna and Mr. Flowers* something that had all the appearances of a murder was actually a suicide. It was a great episode. Lots of twists and turns. And a very relaxing scene set on a farm with cute little cows. Do we think suicide might be possible here?"

"I don't think so," said Miss May. "It would be odd for Buck to have committed suicide in the upstairs bathroom at his place of work in the middle of a busy morning rush. And it would be even stranger for him to commit suicide by eating one bite of a poisoned cinnamon bun or falling with the deliberate intent of hitting his head on the wall and causing a deadly wound."

"I agree," I said. "If Buck was going to commit suicide, he would have done it at home."

"So the guy was murdered," said Miss May. "What does that mean?"

"Well," I said, "Buck was killed sometime between the moment I heard him arguing with Petey and the moment I found him in the bathroom. So chances are the killer was in the restaurant with us. But that's so bizarre. Why would a murderer kill their victim in such a public place?"

"Maybe because murdering someone in a public place is the perfect cover," said Teeny. "Think about it. There were at least 100 people in the restaurant, not including the staff. Any one of them could be guilty. It's like *Where's Waldo?* for catching a killer."

"That's a good point," said Miss May. "One of the guests could have had a secret vendetta against Buck. Or a member of the staff could have done it. It could have been anyone in that place."

"It could have been Petey," I said.

"Petey's soft," said Teeny. "You said so yourself. After Buck yelled at him, the kid broke down into tears."

"What if Petey hardened after that?" I said. "What if he wiped his tears away and decided he had finally had enough so Petey pushed Buck down or fed him the poisoned bun or whatever?"

"I'm not sure if it matters whether or not Buck was pushed or killed by the cinnamon bun," said Miss May. "The simple fact is—"

"I think it matters," I interrupted. "If Buck was pushed down, that's a crime of passion. But if someone went through the trouble to bake poison into a cinnamon bun, that's pre-meditated, which is a whole different set of suspects, motives, everything."

"But how are we going to figure that out?" Teeny asked.

We sat in silence for a moment, stumped. Then I had an idea.

"I think we should try to find out if the staff knew that the upstairs bathroom was out of order," I said. "If everyone knew the bathroom was broken, Buck would have had to have been lured there by the killer."

"Right," said Miss May. "And I think you're correct to suspect the staff. As far as I see it the most likely suspects are disgruntled employees, Petey, or Rebecca, the waitress that entered the bathroom before we left."

"Why Rebecca?" I asked.

Miss May shrugged. "It's possible she was revisiting the scene of the crime to make sure her victim was dead."

"Teeny was seen publicly yelling at Buck yesterday at *Grandma's,* and she was complaining about him with vigor in line this morning. So I think she's going to be a suspect too."

Teeny snorted and rolled her eyes. "That is so ridiculous. I don't kill people. I catch killers!"

"But you can't change the facts," said Miss May. "Chelsea's right. The police are going to flag you as a suspect in this, sooner rather than later."

"So let's hurry up and solve this thing," Teeny said.

"My thoughts exactly." Miss May stood and pulled on her coat. "I think we should talk to Petey first."

8

A FLOOD OF TEARS

*P*etey stood in the center of the dining room at *Land and Sea*, addressing his staff. He spoke in a somber tone and sobbed as he struggled to get through the announcement of Buck's passing.

"I don't know if Petey is cut out to be the owner of a restaurant," I said.

"Sure he is," said Miss May. "He's connecting to his staff. Showing empathy.".

"Maybe we should come back later," said Teeny. "I don't remember Petey being so much of crier. Not that there's anything wrong with that. It's perfectly fine for men to cry. And this is an extreme circumstance."

"You don't have to explain yourself to us," said Miss May. "We know you're not judging anyone. And we also know it's strange that Petey is crying in front of all his employees. Blubbering, really. Can either of you make out any of the words he's saying?"

I leaned forward to try to hear. "I think he said the word kitchen. And maybe he said something about sadness and perseverance? Seems like he's trying to do an emotional, powerful pep talk like in one of those TV shows about high school football coaches."

"Clear eyes, full hearts, can't lose," said Teeny, quoting the classic NBC show, *Friday Night Lights.*

I smirked and look over at her. "You like *Friday Night Lights*?"

"I like Coach Taylor," said Teeny. "He's no Big Dan, don't get me wrong. But I'm a sucker for a strong-willed leader. He got those kids through some tough times and helped them achieve greatness on the grid iron that extended into their personal lives. You've got to admire that."

The group gathered around Petey broke up as Petey concluded his tearful speech. Then the employees trudged toward the exit, mumbling in sadness and dabbing their eyes. Rebecca, the girl who'd walked in on us in the bathroom, shuffled like a zombie, with bedraggled hair and red, puffy cheeks.

"Poor kids are taking this so hard," said Miss May. "Working in a restaurant is already stressful. I can't imagine having to deal with a murdered head chef on top of that."

"Let's talk to Petey." Teeny led the way over to Petey and Miss May and I followed.

Petey let out a big sigh when he saw us coming and gave us a halfhearted wave. "Hi."

"How are you doing, Petey?" Teeny gave Petey a hug and took a step back. "You look terrible. How long have you been crying?"

"Six or seven hours," Petey murmured in a faraway voice. "My eyes hurt."

"I bet they do," said Miss May. She gestured to a nearby table and pulled out a chair. "Take a seat. Let's talk."

Petey nodded. He sat down and buried his head in his hands. "This is terrible."

Teeny put her hand on Petey's arm. "I know. We're all so sorry this happened. It's no secret Buck could be difficult. But you saw him every day and worked with him every day. I'm sure you saw a lot of good in him, despite your differences."

Petey removed his hands from his face and looked over at me. "You told them about the argument."

I gave Petey an apologetic shrug. "Sorry. Buck was so mean and you were crying so much... I couldn't keep it to myself."

"You would have told us anyway, Petey," said Teeny.

Petey shook his head. "Not you. You're my mentor. I want you to think I have my head on straight. That I have every-thing under control. This place is supposed to be successful. And my kitchen is supposed to be a harmonious place, like yours. But I'm a failure."

"You're not a failure," said Teeny.

"My head chef got killed during business hours," said Petey. "He wouldn't listen to anything I said, and he hated my guts."

"Did you hate him as well?" Miss May asked.

Petey sighed. "He disrespected me, and that got on my nerves. And I didn't always agree with his ethics. Like the whole hashbrown lasagna thing. I begged him not to make that dish but he did anyway."

"I knew you wouldn't have stolen my recipe," said Teeny.

"Of course not. But I couldn't totally hate Buck, either. Not even after he stole the recipe. Before I hired him, the restaurant was struggling. I was worried I was going to have to close. But Buck saved this place, so I suppose he deserved to be as arrogant as he wanted."

"Arrogance is a mask for insecurity," I said. "I'm sure Buck hated the fact that you owned the restaurant even though you're so much younger than him. And that's why he treated you with disdain."

"That's what my therapist says," said Petey. "You're smart."

The compliment felt good, even in the midst of tragedy. Although I can be bumbling and clumsy and foolish with stunning regularity, I liked to think I understood people and their feelings pretty well. It felt good for someone to notice that.

"I told my therapist I didn't care that Buck was mean to me. But I did care. I knew it wasn't right for anyone to mistreat me like that, no matter how insecure they might be. There are plenty of chefs in the world. Buck did a good job, sure. But he wasn't so special. A lot of people hated him and that wasn't good for business."

Petey had an angry glint in his eye when he talked about Buck's cooking. He leaned forward in his chair and his speech got faster and faster. "When people start to think they're too good for the place they work that's a problem! When they think they can do whatever they want, no matter what? It's not cool. And it's not right. And it's not fair and it's not right."

Miss May looked at me, concerned. Petey was being manic and repetitive and his vibe was unsettling. But then she turned back to Petey and spoke in a gentle tone. "You're right, Petey. There's never an excuse to be unkind to others. How did you say you found Buck?"

"He answered an ad I placed online," said Petey. "The day he came in for an interview I had twenty great questions prepared. He refused to answer any of them and said he would cook me an omelette instead. The omelette didn't have any fancy truffles or exquisite beef or anything like that. It was simple and it was the best thing I had ever tasted. So I hired him on the spot. I wanted to trust my taste-buds and I thought I was so cool for throwing all my questions away and following my gut. But I was an idiot."

"And how long ago was that?" Miss May asked. "When did you hire Buck?"

"About two months ago," Petey said. "Right before things started to turn around at the restaurant."

Miss May jotted down a few notes then looked back up at Petey. "Can you tell us about the bathroom where Buck was discovered?"

"Was it an employee bathroom?" asked Teeny.

Petey nodded. "Yeah but it's been out of order for a few days, so the staff have been using the downstairs bathroom. That's weird, actually. What was Buck doing up there in the first place?"

"That's a great question, Petey," Miss May said. "And it's a question which we intend to answer."

"Great. Thank you. I'm lucky to have you. All of Pine Grove is lucky to have all three of you." Petey looked down and bit at his thumbnail. "People are going to think I did this, aren't they? The staff is going to talk about the arguments Buck and I used to have. Word's going to travel fast around town. It's not going to be good for me."

"Rumors might spread, sure," said Miss May. "But we aim to catch the killer before any of that becomes a problem for you." She stood. "Thanks for talking to us."

Teeny and I also stood and gathered our things to go. Petey nodded. "Of course. Thank you for talking to me. And for not suspecting me. You don't suspect me do you?"

Teeny gave Petey a small smile. "Of course not, Petey."

Teeny and I exchanged a nervous glance. No matter what Teeny said, it was clear Petey was a prime suspect in this investigation. He had opportunity and he had plenty of motive. And all those tears he cried made him seem unstable if not straight up guilty.

We crossed to the exit but Miss May turned back to Petey just before we left. "Petey? One last question. Do you make cinnamon buns here?"

Petey shook his head. "No. Do you think we should?"

"No," said Miss May. "I wondered, that's all."

9

DOWN TO TOWN

*W*e walked down the hill that led from *Peter's Land and Sea* back to Pine Grove's quaint downtown. It was early evening and we could see the sun setting from on top of the hill. Soft orange light filtered through the gray evening clouds, washing our little village in a calm, warm energy. My shoulders and legs were loose despite the stress of questioning Petey. And based on our slow, relaxed pace, I suspected the sunset was having a similar effect on Teeny and Miss May.

We didn't speak much as we watched the sunset. Then, once the sun disappeared behind a distant hill, Miss May broke the silence. "So what're you girls thinking?"

My aunt's question sent a small wave of excitement through my arms and into my fingertips. We were at the beginning of a new murder investigation. That meant, if all went according to plan, we would have another solved murder on our hands soon. Since I had returned to Pine Grove, I had come to love the thrill of the hunt, the search for answers, and the satisfaction of finding the truth. So I answered Miss May's question before my next footstep hit the ground.

"I think Petey's still on my list of suspects," I said.

"I hate to say it but I agree," said Teeny. "When the kid worked at my restaurant I never pegged him as a killer. Still don't. But he got a little weird when he was talking about Buck back there."

"Right," I said. "His manner changed when he started discussing his relationship with Buck and the dynamics of how they worked together. At first it seemed like Petey was trying to convince us that he needed Buck and that he appreciated Buck's help in revitalizing the business. But the more Petey talked, the angrier he seemed. He started really rambling toward the end there. It was like he chugged an energy drink in the middle of the conversation and got all hopped up."

"By the time he was done ranting, I was convinced Petey hated Buck, despite Petey stating otherwise," said Miss May. "There's no doubt that Petey remains a suspect."

"He seemed genuinely sad when he was talking to the staff though," I said. "I don't know. He's hard to read."

"His emotions have been all over the map for the past couple of days," said Miss May. "He's crying or he's angry or he's burying his head in his hands. We've seen mood swings like that before in guilty killers. It's possible Buck pushed Petey too far and Petey snapped. Perhaps Petey's saddled with a guilty conscience and it's driving him mad."

"The kid is acting weird," said Teeny. "But I've known him for years. I think he has a good heart and I think it would be wise to consider other suspects, at least for now."

"Alright," said Miss May. "You know Petey better than either of us, by far, so I'd like to think you're right. He's always been a nice kid. So what other suspects do we have? What other questions can we ask?"

"I've got an obvious question," I said. "Why was there a cinnamon bun in the bathroom if they don't even make cinnamon buns there?"

Teeny shrugged. "I've traveled with cinnamon buns before. Maybe Buck brought it from home."

Miss May shifted her weight from side to side. "I might believe that if he didn't work in a kitchen. But why bother baking at home when you can make the mess at work and have someone else clean it up?"

"Good point," said Teeny.

"I think we need to talk to that waitress, Rebecca," said Miss May. "We need to find out why she was headed to an upstairs bathroom that the staff knew was out of order. And maybe she'll be able to shed some light on the mystery of the cinnamon bun, too."

We came to the bottom of the hill and Pine Grove's Main Street unfolded before us. The town lawyer, Tom Gigley, hurried into his office with a pizza. The owner of the town coffee shop, Brian, chatted with a few patrons on the sidewalk in front of his business, complaining loudly about his broken espresso machine. And two little old ladies climbed into a sensible sedan, each holding a big bouquet of flowers.

As I looked out over the townspeople, I remembered why it was so important for us to solve this murder. I wanted to keep our town safe from danger, and the best way to do that was to catch the killer, of course.

Then a second, darker thought crossed my mind. One of the people out on the street in front of me could be the murderer. And we needed to find out who it was, before someone else turned up dead.

10

REBECCA DE MOURNING

I woke up the next morning to the smell of dark, home brewed coffee. The second the scent hit my nose, my feet plopped out of the bed and walked me down to the kitchen without my consent. My groggy eyes spotted a vaguely Miss May-shaped being over by the counter. My head gave the humanoid being a little nod and my throat grunted a sound intended to communicate the sentiment, "good morning." Finally, my hands poured me a cup of coffee and brought it to my lips.

As soon as at first sip hit my lips, the world came into focus. This Miss May-shaped being was Miss May. The sky outside was gray. And, in my sleep stupor, I had forgotten to add cream and sugar to my cup of joe.

When I had first moved to Pine Grove, I hadn't been much of a coffee drinker. I hadn't been a big fan of the taste and I'd been really trying to limit my caffeine intake. For the longest time, any cup I consumed needed more cream than coffee and more sugar than cream. But there was something about finding dead bodies and investigating murders that made me want to drink stronger coffee and talk fast and say,

"Look here!" like a P.I. in a black and white movie. As a former New York City prosecutor, Miss May had always preferred her coffee strong and black, but I was still working on my toughness.

I added a splash of cream and a sprinkle of sugar to my cup, then turned my focus over to Miss May. She gave me a smile. "Are you fully operational yet or do you need more coffee?"

"I'm powering up." I sat at the kitchen table and took another sip. "I'd say the system is at about 60% but that's as good as we're going to do for the foreseeable future, so we might as well start talking."

"Sure. Let's see, what can we talk about? I had a wonderful morning. I went over the books with KP at around 5 AM. Turns out we had a strong, profitable apple picking season. Sold five percent more apple cider donuts that we did last year, which I think we can attribute to the new signage. At around 6 AM, I went into the bakeshop and prepped some dough for pie crust. That reminds me, we got a big order for pies that I need you to help me fill at some point. Then I watched the news and pet Kitty for a while. Steve the dog looked pretty jealous while I was petting the cat so at the commercial break I took him for a walk across the orchard. He stopped by the stream and played for a few minutes. I don't know how the cold water doesn't matter to dogs. That's what fur is for, I guess. Anyway, now I'm here looking at my zombie niece as she joins the land of the living."

"I don't like it when you rub your productivity in my face. It makes me feel like I should be doing more around the farm."

"Are you saying you want to do more around the farm?"

I laughed. "I do plenty."

"I know," Miss May said with a grin. "More than enough. I don't know where I would be without your help."

"I solve a lot of mysteries too, you know. It's not all farm work and apple pies in my life."

Miss May chuckled. "You don't say? That is so impressive. Are you working on any cases right now?"

"As a matter of fact, I'm headed to interview a new suspect this morning. She lives in the next town over, so I don't know her well but I'm interested to find out more."

Miss May took a sip of her coffee, then set it down. "Alright. Enough joking around. Let's head over to Blue Mountain to so we can catch Rebecca with her guard down at home."

"How you know she's not going to be at *Peter's Land and Sea*?"

"I looked at the calendar in Petey's office. Monday is Rebecca's day off. Also... The chef was murdered so I doubt they're open."

I winced. "I'll drive."

We picked Teeny up from *Grandma's* and headed off to find Rebecca. Miss May called around to a few friends as we headed over toward the little town of Blue Mountain, New York. It only took two or three calls for Miss May to find out Rebecca's exact address. *That's life in a small town for ya!* So I plugged the information into my phone and my GPS took us straight to her front door.

Rebecca lived in a small community of cottages situated near a tiny lake. Her home was brick, one-story and from the looks of it, very small. There were a few rusty old bicycles leaning near the front door and part of the roof had been patched with a blue tarp.

"Are you sure this is the right address?" I asked.

"Yeah, it's a dump," Teeny said.

Miss May shrugged. "Sadly, servers don't often make enough to live in giant countryside estates. This is the right spot."

Rebecca answered the door with a grimace. "What are the three of you doing here? You're the people who found Buck's body."

"You remember us. Terrific. May we come inside?" Miss May moved to enter the house. I expected Rebecca to resist but she stepped aside and allowed us to pass.

The inside of the home was decorated in a tasteful and modern aesthetic. There was a glass coffee table with gold legs and a large piece of trendy, modern art. A copper French press rested on the table.

"This place is nice," I said. "I like your artwork."

"You're surprised that it's not a dump," said Rebecca.

"Yeah I was expecting…" Teeny started. "Not a dump. Nevermind."

"The outside needs some work. Those bicycles and all that other trash belong to my landlord. I refuse to clean it up until he fixes all the problems I have in the house. Starting with the hole in the roof. Anyway. What are you three doing here?"

"We wanted to talk about Buck," said Miss May.

"I don't have a lot of time." Rebecca opened up a laptop and started typing with impressive speed. "I run a business on the side. And I'm way behind on emails. I'm trying to use this time off from the restaurant to catch up on my backlog."

"What's your side business?" I asked.

Rebecca muttered as she typed, ignoring my question. She glanced up and noticed we were all three staring at her expectantly.

"So what's up?" Rebecca asked. "Do you like, want to

start a support group for people who saw the dead body in the bathroom? I still don't understand why you're here."

Miss May, Teeny, and I exchanged wide-eyed glances. We'd solved so many murders in the area, we'd grown accustomed to our reputation preceding us. Suspects almost always knew why we wanted to talk to them as soon as we arrived at their homes. But we had a unique opportunity with Rebecca, because she had no idea that we were investigating the crime.

"You're right," said Miss May. "Discovering that body upset us all so much. You were also in the room that day. We thought if we could talk to you, somehow we might find closure, so we might be able to move past this devastating tragedy. We didn't know uh...Buck, was that his name?"

"That's right," said Rebecca, still typing.

"We didn't know him. But none of us can shake the image of his body from our minds. Did you know him well?"

"Yeah, you seemed upset when we were all crammed in that little bathroom with his corpse," Teeny said. "Were you two close?"

Rebecca kept typing on her laptop without looking up. Miss May cleared her throat. "Did you know Buck well?"

"Yeah, I'm sorry, I can't do this. The whole, talk about your emotions thing? I stopped with that nonsense after my first therapy session in high school. Buck is no longer with us, right? No point thinking about it. No point fixating on the image of his lifeless corpse in your mind. You've just got to move on and keep living life."

I stammered. "Wow, that's..."

"Cold? Calculating? Heartless?" Rebecca suggested.

"Uh, well, you have an impressive grip on your emotions," I said. "Is that something you've cultivated thanks to working in the restaurant business? Or because of your other business on the side? What did you say that was again?"

"Nothing. Sales." Rebecca muttered as she clicked around on her computer. "People are so hard to work with sometimes. I hate customers. I hate suppliers. I hate everyone but me."

"I'm sorry to hear that," said Miss May. She reached into her purse and pulled out an apple pie. "I'm a baker. I don't know if you like apple pies but—"

"No pies for me, thank you. I don't like eating. And I don't really like you three either. No offense, it's not personal. Remember that thing I said about hating everyone but me? That applies to the three of you as well. This whole conversation is making me feel weird. Most importantly, I have tons of work I need to do."

Rebecca jumped to her feet, crossed to the door and held it open for us to leave. "Do me a favor and never come back."

Miss May set the pie down on Rebecca's coffee table. "I'll leave that there. My card is taped to the top of the box if you ever need to talk. Or want another pie."

Seconds later, Miss May, Teeny, and I were back outside Rebecca's house. It had begun to rain and thunder clapped overhead. On the surface, it seemed we hadn't gotten much out of our interview. But I had a feeling that Rebecca hadn't told us the whole truth. And I wanted to find out why.

11

CHELSEA THE TRASH PICKER

*T*he downtown of Blue Mountain, New York was small but cute. There was a general store that sold everything from fishing tackle to milk and eggs. The post office was housed in a brick building that looked smaller than my Jersey City apartment. And there was a tiny park, the shape of a thumbprint, with a little pond in its center.

Miss May and Teeny talked in excited tones about how strange our visit to Rebecca had been. Teeny, apparently, had noticed that Rebecca's kitchen was a little messy, even though the rest of the house was clean. Teeny theorized that Rebecca might be a sloppy eater, or a messy cook. Miss May hadn't noticed the kitchen and therefore didn't have much to add. The discussion of the kitchen occupied most of the drive from Rebecca's house down into the town of Blue Mountain.

I pulled into a parking spot in front of the general store and slammed my sky blue pickup into park. "Enough about the kitchen. We need to talk about this case."

Teeny leaned forward. "But did you see the kitchen? If

you saw it, I think you'd have something to say. Really didn't go with the rest of the house. The whole place had a weird mismatched vibe. The outside said, 'a homeless person lives here,' but the inside said, 'I'm not homeless, this is my home.'"

I looked at Teeny sideways. She had a unique way with words.

"Rebecca says all that stuff outside belongs to the landlord," said Miss May. "Are you suggesting the landlord was also responsible for her sloppy kitchen?"

Teeny tightened her jaw. "Please stop condescending to me. I'm an expert sleuth. It's not my fault I observed a detail the two of you missed."

"I suppose I was too busy noticing Rebecca's generally suspicious behavior," said Miss May. "She barely looked up from her computer. Her left leg fidgeted throughout our conversation. And I'm not sure she and I made eye contact once."

"She didn't make eye contact with me, either," I said.

"She also didn't tell us anything about her business, despite her preoccupation with emails the whole time," Teeny said. "I tell you, it is so rude to work on emails when you have company. It's not the right way to treat a guest, even if the guest is at your house because they suspect you killed the head chef at the restaurant where you work."

I pulled out my phone. "Let's see what we can find out online about Rebecca's side business."

"Good idea," Miss May said. "The more we learn about Rebecca the more we might begin to understand her means, her potential motive, and this murder."

"What are you going to search?" Teeny asked. "Try 'Rebecca sketchy side business, Blue Mountain, New York.'"

I laughed. "You don't use the Internet often, do you?"

Teeny gave me a big grin. "I'm a Luddite."

As soon as I began to type a search into the web browser my phone screen went black. I groaned. "No. No, no, no. I swear my phone despises me. Every time I need it, it dies. Can I use one of your phones?"

Miss May bit her lip. "I didn't bring mine. It's too heavy. It weighs down my pants."

"Miss May. We need it." I turned to Teeny. "What about you? I suppose it's crazy to think you'd have your phone."

"Yup! I only take my phone out of the house if there's going to be an emergency."

"How do you know when there's going to be an emergency?" I asked.

Teeny opened her mouth to speak but stopped before she formed any words. "That's a good point. I never really plan on having an emergency. That's why I never take my phone out of the house."

"It's OK, Chelsea," said Miss May. "Don't let your delicate Millennial heart break for no reason. We'll get the information we need the old-fashioned way." Miss May patted the steering wheel a few times. "Start this puppy up. We're going back to Rebecca's."

"We can't break into her house," I protested in a slightly whiny tone. "She's home and she's angry for no reason."

"We're not breaking in," Miss May said with a twinkle in her eye. "We're digging through her trash."

We rolled back into Rebecca's neighborhood nice and slow and parked about two blocks away from her home so she wouldn't spot us on the approach. I hopped out of the car upon our arrival, but neither Teeny nor Miss May budged. When I poked my head back in the car of the two of them were twiddling their thumbs, looking as innocent as newborn lambs.

"Let's go," I said.

"Digging through trash isn't a task suited for elderly women, Chelsea." Miss May said, as though it was the most obvious statement in the world. "It's your job to gather this particular piece of evidence."

I threw up my hands. "I've already been in a dumpster once this week!"

"Practice makes perfect," Teeny said.

"Oh come on. Miss May has way longer arms than me!"

"I'm also much larger and more conspicuous than you," Miss May countered.

"You've dug through trash before! In the Hamptons!" I said, not willing to give up without a fight.

"That was at an empty house. No one around to spot my hulking girth," Miss May said.

"Oh you're not hulking or girthy!" I said. "You're just saying that."

Miss May shrugged and I could see there was no use arguing. So I took a deep breath and let it out, long and slow. "Fine. I'll be back soon."

The second I closed the door to the pickup and turned to face Rebecca's neighborhood, I realized I was all alone in the world on a desperate hunt for trash. That meant that I needed to be stealthy in order to succeed in my mission. Rebecca's house was at the other end of the street, but I didn't want to be seen on the approach so I snuck into the backyard of one of her neighbors' homes. For some reason, it felt important not to make any sound, so I entered the small patch of forest that connected one backyard to another on my tiptoes.

Once I was five feet into the forest I noticed all the new sounds around me. Birds chirping, squirrels scampering through fallen leaves. Somewhere in the distance a stream seemed to gurgle out the words, "Chelsea the Trash Picker. Chelsea the Trash Picker." *Wasn't the worst epithet I'd been called.*

I hurried through the woods toward Rebecca's house and moments later I could see her side window from where I stood. Rebecca was in the kitchen, which looked clean to me, preparing herself a sandwich for lunch.

I hid behind a tree until she sat down at the kitchen table to eat. Then I started for the side yard, in search of the garbage can.

Chelsea the Trash Picker was good at her job. An enormous garbage can was propped up against the house, teeming with refuse.

"Jackpot," I said, as if popping an enormous safe during a bank robbery.

I peeked through a nearby window. Rebecca was hard at work on what appeared to be a turkey and cheese sandwich. She was distracted by her lunch, as any sane woman would be, but I needed to be quiet in order to remain under the radar.

I lifted the lid to the garbage can and it thumped gently against the house. When I looked back inside Rebecca was still enjoying a romantic moment with her sandwich but I knew that the thumping lid was strike one. I had to be extra careful. So I turned back to the garbage with gentle, precise movements, again conjuring the image of a stealthy bank robber on the job.

The oversized trash bin was filled with several bags of garbage, each individually tied. I opened the first bag and a few empty soda cans spilled to the ground. It was way too loud. I flattened myself against the house and tried to remain unseen and silent.

Seconds later, I heard Rebecca's footsteps approaching

the window. I could hear Rebecca groaning as she tried to open the window from the inside.

The sound of an idling engine pulled my attention over to the street. It was Teeny and Miss May, ready to make an escape in the getaway car.

Rebecca cursed as she fought the window and I heard it begin to open.

I realized that was my moment to take action so I grabbed the overflowing bag of trash from the top of the garbage bin, slung it over my shoulder and darted toward the pickup. Miss May's eyes widened as I ran toward her, trash spilling out behind me like exhaust on an old diesel clunker. My heart raced as I got close to the pickup truck and tossed the trash bag into the bed.

"Hurry up," said Miss May. "We need to get out of here."

Trying to expedite our departure, I climbed onto the wheel well and hoisted my stumpy little body into the bed of the pickup truck, landing with a resounding clunk right beside the pile of trash.

Miss May pulled out with a squeal. I tossed my head back, closed my eyes and sighed. Part of me felt like that entire debacle had been pointless.

But I couldn't have been more wrong. And you're about to find out why.

12

APOTHECARY NOW

*A*bout an hour later, Miss May, Teeny and I were back at the farmhouse staring down an enormous pile of trash. We'd spread out a tarp and laid all the trash out flat, which made for a smelly and repulsive sight. There were food wrappers and crumpled papers and takeout containers and tissues... It was disgusting. But all in a day's work for a team of amateur sleuths.

"Alright," said Miss May. "Let's get to work and see if we can find anything suspicious."

Teeny clamped a clothes pin down on her nose then offered an identical clothes pin to both me and Miss May. "Clothes pin?"

Miss May and I laughed. The laugh lasted probably a full minute, and the whole time Teeny looked at us like she wasn't crazy at all for snapping her nostrils shut with a clothes pin.

After the laughing finally died down Teeny gave us an oblivious shrug. "What are you two laughing at?" Her voice was so high-pitched and nasally we cracked up laughing again. Then, after Teeny explained that the clothes pin kept the stench out of her nose, Miss May and I each begrudgingly accepted one of our own clothes pins. It did help a little, but we must've looked absolutely insane as we dug through the smelly trash pile.

For ten straight minutes, all any of us found was literal trash. Then I found a small piece of paper that seemed promising. I handed it to Miss May. "Look at this. It seems like an invoice for Rebecca's business."

"Let's see here." Miss May put on her glasses. "Hard to tell much of anything past all these mustard stains."

"Look at the top of the paper," I said. "See? It's a thousand dollar bill sent from some big company in New Jersey to a company in Blue Mountain."

"And you think that Blue Mountain company is Rebecca's side business?" Teeny asked.

Miss May let out a long, deep sigh. "That theory makes sense to me. You girls ready for another adventure?"

I grinned. "Always."

The address on the invoice led us to a cluster of large, square buildings nestled along one of Blue Mountain's many wooded back roads. Each building had a large garage door that took up most of the façade, with another small door on the side. The whole area had a dark and intense energy, like the kind of place a Bond villain would hide his secret weapon. There were no cars in the parking lot and there wasn't another soul in sight.

"I don't like this place," said Teeny. "It feels evil. Like it's storage specifically for criminals to hide their dirty secrets."

"I thought the same thing," I said. "This place gives me a bad feeling. And it doesn't look like a business park. It looks like a boring storage facility."

Miss May shook her head. "You can't get mail to your storage unit. These units must be zoned commercial. Sometimes people use garages like this as autobody shops or warehouses that double as retail spaces, stuff like that."

"What kind of business do you think Rebecca runs out of here?" Teeny asked. "What if she's selling black market organs or something?"

"I doubt she'd have invoices for her organ business," I said.

"Hey, even illegal organ dealers need to stay organized," Teeny replied. "Gotta keep track of your livers somehow!"

"What unit is she?" Miss May asked.

I checked the paper from the trash. Its wet mustard smell burned my nose. "Unit 109C."

"Let's go," said Miss May.

We soon found ourselves at the entrance of Unit 109C. By all appearances, it was just like every other unit. We tried the large garage door and the side door but they were both locked.

"No way in," Teeny said. "What do we do now?"

"Hold on a second." I spotted a small window above the door on the side of the building. It looked as if it was slightly ajar. "Give me a boost and I bet I can climb through that."

Miss May and Teeny both looked at me like I had a thousand heads and peanut butter eyeballs. "You can't climb on us," said Miss May. "Our bones will disintegrate."

"Oh they will not," I said. "You're not centuries old. You've got sturdy bones."

"I have osteoporosis," Teeny said. "My doctor specifically said, don't let young people climb on your shoulders."

"Why would your doctor... You know what, nevermind," I tossed Miss May the keys to the pickup. "Pull Glenn Close under the window and I'll climb on top."

"Your pickup is called Glenn Close now?"

"Sure."

Moments later, I flopped from the roof of the pickup in through the window and landed on a high shelf in a large, dark room. I used the flashlight on my phone to look around. The room was organized in a neat fashion, similar to Rebecca's home. The shelves were lined with a multitude of jars that contained strange, viscous fluids, powders and other compounds.

"Are you in?" Teeny called from outside.

"Of course she's in. We know that because she's not out anymore," said Miss May.

"She knows what I mean," said Teeny. "Are you OK?"

"I'm fine." I took a closer look at the unit. Lots of the jars were shaped like old-timey chemist beakers. And a pleasant floral smell permeated the space. That's when it hit me... "I think this might be storage for some kind of apothecary or something."

"An apothecary?" Teeny asked. "Like from the 1800s?"

"Apothecaries are trendy again," I said. "Before I moved back here from New York City, there was a hipster apothecary popping up in every neighborhood. They're basically glorified, overpriced drugstores. They would sell body butter or organic shampoo and perfumes, stuff like that. And the whole place would be decorated like a chemistry lab or something. One of the many ridiculous retail trends in the city. Possibly the most ridiculous. I guess Rebecca is trying to bring the trend up here."

"Thanks for the education, Chelsea, but can you let us in?" Miss May asked.

I shimmied down the shelf toward the floor. About thirty seconds later, I was sweaty and my arms and legs were tired but my feet were on the floor. I opened the side door and Teeny and Miss May entered and flipped on the lights.

Teeny walked from shelf to shelf, looking at all of the

tinctures and powders and creams. "What is all this stuff?"
She picked up a light jar of pink cream and smelled it. "It
smells amazing. Like rose petals."

Miss May browsed the labels on the bottles and jars,
reading ingredients. "Turbines. Glycols. Synthetic colors.
Synthetic fragrances. Sodium sulfate. Thyme. Argan oil.
Lion's mane. Cassava." She turned back to me. "It seems like
Rebecca's apothecary is a not-so-healthy mix of chemicals
and natural ingredients."

"That's better than most of the big companies," I said.
"They just stick to chemicals."

Miss May pointed at a large, locked cabinet across the
room. "All the expensive ingredients must be in there." She
walked toward the cabinet and pulled at an enormous
padlock. "Unless there's something else in there?" Miss May
turned back and looked at me and Teeny. "Something
diabolical."

"Seems like somebody who knows so much about chemicals and tinctures might be a good candidate to mix up a
poison," I said.

"Maybe," said Miss May, "but there's no arsenic in here.
No cyanide. No proof."

"So what do we do now?" I asked.

Miss May shrugged. "Now we look for proof."

13

POISON APPLES

*Y*ou know that feeling when you're looking for something and then you finally find it and you feel so good? Like it's the best news you've ever gotten?

Miss May, Teeny and I did not have the luxury of enjoying that feeling that night in Rebecca's unit. Although we searched for hours, we didn't turn up any evidence that suggested Rebecca might have killed Buck. So we left late at night, I think it was almost 11 PM, with our heads hung low and our stomachs rumbling.

When Miss May and I arrived back at the farm that night, Wayne was sitting on the porch steps, leaning back on his elbows with his feet crossed at the ankles.

Miss May turned to me. "Looks like somebody has a special visitor."

My face reddened. "I'm sure he's just here about the foot."

"That's what all the girls say."

"That doesn't even make sense."

Miss May chuckled, got out of the car and gave Wayne a big wave. "Detective Hudson. It's a pleasure to see you looking so relaxed. How are you this fine October evening? Do you have a case of the Mondays or are you feeling great?"

Wayne stood at attention. "Miss May, hi. Sorry I was lounging. I've just been waiting here for... A while. A good, long while. I tried Chelsea's phone but it's dead and I presume you don't have yours with you?"

"I don't."

I sidled up behind Miss May and tried my best to give off a cool and confident vibe. "What's up Wayne? How you doing?"

"I'm OK, thanks. Hope you're doing well too."

"You're here to see Chelsea?" Miss May asked.

"No. I've got news about the case, that's all."

Miss May looked back at me and winked. Then she turned back to Wayne. "I need to head inside. My dogs are barkin'. You two stay out here in the moonlight and discuss all that needs to be discussed. Chelsea will catch me up later."

Miss May brushed past Wayne and entered the farm-house with what I was sure was a glib little smile. The screen door closed behind her and suddenly I was alone, with only Wayne and the faraway sound of an owl singing in the night.

Neither Wayne nor I talked for a few seconds. Then we both spoke at the same time.

"I'm sorry, go ahead," said Wayne.

"No. You go," I said. "There's news about the case?"

Wayne nodded. "Right. Right. I'm here about the case." I narrowed my eyes. *Was he telling me that or was that some-*

thing he was telling himself? "Yeah. Big news back from the lab. Turns out Buck didn't die from a head wound."

"What did he die from?" I asked. "Actually, hold on a second. Why are you telling me this? Chief Flanagan hates me and Miss May and Teeny. And you're not often so giving with information."

"Do you want me not to tell you?"

"No. I— Of course I want to know. I'm just confused."

Wayne looked down and nudged the earth with his shoe. "I get that. And you're right. I'm not usually so giving. But I'm trying to turn over a new leaf. Look, you and Miss May and even Teeny, you've been helpful. The fact of the matter is we've got a murder problem in this town. And the three of you are a big part of what I see as the solution. I've decided that what Chief Flanagan doesn't know won't hurt her. So I'm sharing my information with you. That's what's best for Pine Grove and I'm not going to let my ego get in the way." Wayne's eyes met mine. "I know you don't like guys with big egos."

That last sentence hung in the air for a few seconds. I wondered if Wayne was truly changing his tune for the benefit of the people of Pine Grove or if, perhaps, he was changing his tune to draw me away from Germany Turtle. Either way, I didn't mind it.

I stood a little taller. "OK. I respect that. Miss May and Teeny will appreciate that you've decided to clue us in, so to speak. But I can't promise we're going to reciprocate. No offense, but the Pine Grove Police Department has a bit of a habit of bungling investigations. Half the time Flanagan won't even admit there's been a murder until we're halfway finished solving the crime. If we have an important clue and the wrong officer gets a hold of it... Who knows what could happen?"

"I expect you'll use your discretion and share whatever you think you can," said Wayne.

"You expect correct."

"Anyway," said Wayne, "the reason I'm here is because we found out that Buck didn't die from his head wound. Maybe you and your aunt already suspected that, but... we've confirmed that the injury was incidental. There was blood but it wasn't a deep gash. Buck could have walked away from his fall without even getting stitches. The guy died from poison, turns out. Not sure how they determined that, I don't know the science. But yeah, that's what got him. Poison in that delicious looking cinnamon bun. I think the medical examiner said it was 'technically cyanide?' Don't know what was technical about it. Weird. But, this is important to note, we can now conclude—"

"That this was not an impulsive crime of passion," I interrupted. "Whoever did this planned it out ahead of time. They didn't get angry at Buck and slam his head into the tile. They pre-meditated the killing, cold and meticulous."

"Took the words right off my lips." I tried not to look at Wayne's lips as he said that. *But they were quite plump and luscious.*

I moved past Wayne and toward the door to the farmhouse. "Alright. Thanks for stopping by."

Wayne stepped in my path. "Wait. I've got another question. About um, I guess another type of investigation?"

I looked at him and blinked like a wide-eyed ingenue as if to say, *I'm waiting.* I didn't know why but I was feeling sassy and I liked it.

"OK," Wayne continued. "So basically I'm wondering... What's the deal with you and Germany Turtle?"

"He's my boyfriend. He's in Africa. That's public knowledge."

"Right. But I'm after the private knowledge. Seems to me the guy's pretty committed to petting those Saharan lions or whatever. Watching them while they sleep. Hey, I'm sure it's important work. It is what it is. I just want to know how you feel about it. Attractive, successful city girl like you... She shouldn't be abandoned for a pride of lions, if you ask me."

Wayne had some nerve, making assumptions about my relationship. Even if he was a little right. Germany had won me over with his persistence and endearing verbosity and constant presence. So yeah, sure, long distance had a been challenge. But we were making it work. *Right?*

"Enough about Germany," I said, sidestepping Wayne's questions. "Back to this murder in Pine Grove. That should be the focus of your concern. And I have a question of my own. Are the cops looking at Teeny as a suspect?"

Wayne shrugged. "You don't want to talk to me, I don't want to talk to you."

"I thought you wanted to share information all of a sudden!"

"All of a sudden now I don't."

"Uch. Whatever. Can you at least tell me what's going on with that foot?"

Wayne squinted into the darkness and acted like he was in a film noir. "No can do, ma'am. Official police business."

As Wayne drove away I thought about our conversation. He'd clammed up the moment I'd refused to talk about Germany. But I felt a strange bubbling sensation through my torso. It was almost as if... I liked that Wayne had acted jealous.

I sat on the porch steps and let out a long, slow breath. My mind flashed to images of the cinnamon bun with one bite taken out, and then to the severed foot that Steve the dog had dug up on the orchard. Life in Pine Grove seemed

simple on its face. But small town living was more complicated than it looked on the surface.

A heavy dread replaced the bubbling in my stomach.
Miss May, Teeny, and I had work to do... Because there was
no telling who might turn up dead next.

14

DOG TIRED

*A*fter a few minutes, I went into the farmhouse and headed up the stairs to my bedroom. Steve the dog was curled up on my comforter. He lifted his head when I entered and his ears shifted with alert curiosity. His tail wagged as I approached.

I smiled, happy to see him. Then, we had a true heart-to-heart conversation. I spoke aloud, of course. But Steve communicated entirely with his big, expressive eyes. The following is a transcript of that conversation:

Me: "Hey, Steve. You look comfortable. Any room on that dog bed for a human?"

Steve: "Sure. But try not to make me move."

Me: "Thanks. It's so kind of you to allow me a little space on my own bed."

Steve: "Anytime."

There were a few minutes of silence after I flopped down on the bed, then Steve rearranged himself so his head was on my stomach. He was warm and soft and I stroked the soft fur of his back. Then he looked up at me with his big, brown eyes.

Steve: "What's going on with you? I sense some angst or discomfort in your belly region. I don't think it's gas because I don't hear anything."

Me: "You need a haircut."

Steve: "Don't change the subject. I want to know what's going on with you. You're always afraid to confront your emotions head on. It's not good."

Me: "I've got a lot on my mind. Leave me alone."

There were a few more moments of silence as I ran my head over Steve's long coat. *He really did need a haircut.*

But Steve just couldn't move on...

Steve: "Is this about Germany? What's your status with him, anyway? It seems like he might love lions more than he loves you."

Me: "That's not nice."

Steve: "Relax. You know what I mean. The guy's in Africa all the time. Why do the lions need to be studied? They're the kings and queens of the jungle. They're fine without some Turtle sitting around watching their every move."

Me: "I admire his research. It's nice that he wants to help the lions."

Steve: "But that's what I'm saying... How does he want to help them?"

Me: "I don't know. I guess you're right. I do feel confused about my status with Germany. He's my boyfriend, I know that. But Wayne has been sending me some strong signals, and I guess that's making me... confused."

Steve: "I get that. You and Wayne have a thing. He has a really strong man smell, I always notice it. How do you feel about Wayne?"

I shrugged. Steve whined. I rolled my eyes.

Me: "I like him. You know that I like him. You've witnessed our conversations on several occasions. We have chemistry. He's handsome. That doesn't mean we have to be an item. Especially because I'm spoken for."

Steve: "That's not a very feminist term. You shouldn't be spoken for. You should do the speaking."

Me: "You know what I mean."

Steve rolled over on his belly and I scratched it. Then he flipped back over onto his stomach and looked at me.

Steve: "Do you think Teeny is going to be arrested?"

Me: "I don't know. I hope not. But these cops have done stupider things."

Steve: "What do you think about the whole cinnamon bun thing?"

Me: "It's a disgrace! Who would kill someone with something as delicious as a cinnamon bun? It's a crime against baked goods everywhere! When we catch this killer, they should get an extra stern punishment for ruining that cinnamon bun. I don't know if I'm ever going to be able to eat a cinnamon bun again, come to think of it. They're all going to look like poison to me. What a tragedy."

Steve: "There's no way you're staying away from cinnamon buns forever."

Me: "You know me too well."

I fell asleep a few minutes later with Steve curled up in the nook of my arm.

As I slept, I dreamt that Miss May, Teeny, and I were running through the streets of Pine Grove pursuing a masked criminal. Just as we caught up to the criminal, they jumped in a bright red convertible and disappeared into the night. The driver tossed poisonous cinnamon buns out the window as they sped away.

In the dream, I felt frustrated and slow, like in those nightmares where you're trying to run and every muscle in your body feels like molasses.

But when I woke up the next morning the nightmare didn't hang with me in a bad way. Instead, it motivated me to get out of bed and get to work solving the case. There was a lot Miss May, Teeny and I needed to discuss, and it was important that we act fast.

15

MORNING WALKS

I shuffled into the kitchen around 8 AM to find a handwritten note on the counter that read "Wanted to get my exercise. Walked over to *Grandma's*." I shook my head. *Grandma's* was at least three miles from the farm, which was a long distance for my aunt. And did Miss May expect me to walk just because she had? There was no chance of that happening. So I jumped in my light blue pickup and drove into town.

My radio was broken so I sang along to the song in my head. The tune was mostly about the pretty leaves on the trees and my need for Big Dan to fix my radio. I secretly hoped he would do it for cheap because he was Teeny's love interest. But deep down I knew I'd pay any price for the ability to blast *REO Speedwagon* at top volume on my way into town again.

The parking lot at *Grandma's* was empty so I grabbed the spot right out front and jaunted inside. I hadn't forgotten my conversation with Steve the dog, and I was ready to get going so we could crack our case wide open.

When I entered, the homestyle restaurant had that cozy

"opening up for the day" vibe. A hunched-over waitress married the ketchups at a table. A teenage girl vacuumed the floors, dancing a little bit to whatever music played in her headphones. Teeny's mom, Granny, sat at the cash register doing a crossword puzzle. And Miss May and Teeny were seated in our booth, each sipping a cup of coffee, with a mostly empty pot in front of them.

Miss May raised her eyebrows when she saw me. "Chelsea. You made it. Don't tell me you walked too."

I tossed my keys down on the table and sat next to Teeny. "No way, Miss May. I figured you did enough exercise for both of us this morning."

"Is that how that works?" Miss May asked with a smirk.

"Yup."

Teeny chuckled. "If that's the case you exercised for me, too, May. Thanks for that. You're the best."

Teeny flagged down a waiter and asked for a fresh pot of coffee. Then she and Miss May resumed their conversation, gossiping about a friend who had moved to Florida and found herself with two boyfriends. Although that conversation would have riveted me in the past, on that morning I had little patience for trivial matters such as the extracurricular love affairs of the septuagenarian snowbirds.

"This is all fascinating," I said, "but we have more important things to discuss."

"Good point." Teeny leaned forward. "I also need to tell you about my cousin's cousin's best friend's neighbor. She moved to Arizona instead of Florida and says the food is just OK."

I laughed. "Teeny. We need to talk about the case."

"You mean the case of detective Wayne making a late-night visit to Chelsea Thomas?" Miss May grinned. "We already covered that."

Miss May and Teeny giggled in perfect unison.

"What would you two do without gossip?" I asked. "How would you fill the hours?"

"We'd find something to talk about," said Teeny. "We always do. And I'd probably just watch more British crime shows, honestly."

"Well, right now we're living an American crime show," I said. "And we need to figure out what we're going to do next. Petey seems innocent but he had motive and opportunity. Maybe Petey tricked Buck, said the upstairs bathroom was working again, then followed him up there and shoved that cinnamon bun in Buck's mouth."

"Possible," said Miss May. "Although that would be an odd way to poison someone. If it were me, I would've just found out Buck's favorite sweet treat, baked some poison into it and waited for him to take the bait."

Teeny pointed at Miss May. "Exactly. Trap that rat with his favorite flavor poison. I bet that's how the killer did it. Buck was such a greedy, hideous monster of a man, may he rest in peace. I'm sure he couldn't resist any temptation, whatsoever. Did I say may he rest in peace?"

Miss May nodded. "Yeah. But I don't know if that makes the rest of what you said any nicer."

"I just want to show my respect," said Teeny. "But I can't help how I feel."

"Don't talk about it so loud though," I said. "If the people in Pine Grove hear you calling Buck a greedy monster, they're going to start thinking you committed the murder. And if the tide of public opinion turns against you, the cops may take action. They've arrested us for less in the past."

"KP, too," said Miss May, referring to her trusty farm-hand who'd been accused of murder by the PGPD not long ago. "From now on, if you want to say something nasty about Buck, turn every mean word into a nice word."

"I can do that. Let me try right now..." Teeny cleared her throat. "I... loved... Buck. The fact that he stole my recipes delighted me. I loved it any time I saw his handsome and beautiful face. And let's not forget about his chiseled, trim body. That guy was wonderful. Whenever I saw him I wanted to give him a big... hug right around the neck. I wanted to hug him so hard he lives forever."

Miss May and I exchanged a concerned glance. Teeny perked up with a big smile. "Well. That felt great. Thanks."

"Sometimes you scare me," said Miss May. "What other suspects do we have?"

"I mean, there's Rebecca," I ventured, but I couldn't keep the skepticism from my voice when I said her name. "She was up in the bathroom even though it didn't work, which was odd. And she was hostile to us, for sure. But she was busy with her side business, which I understand. I can't find the motive there."

"Hostile people sometimes commit murder," said Miss May.

"I know. But does Rebecca seem like the type to poison a cinnamon bun? She's so impatient and rough around the edges. If she was ever going to murder someone I bet it would be a crime of passion. Maybe blunt force trauma over the back of the head or perhaps a stabbing? Nothing so gentle as a cinnamon bun. And not as delicious, either."

Miss May turned down the sides of her mouth, impressed. "Wow. You're getting good at this, Chelsea. I agree with your reasoning completely."

"Not me," said Teeny. "The woman has a storage unit filled with possible poisons! That's an important clue. She also seems like a poisoner to me. When I see her walking on the street, I think, 'You poison people.' That's her vibe, I've always thought so."

Miss May waved Teeny away. "You have not."

"It doesn't matter, anyway," I said. "We're not taking Rebecca off the table as a suspect. Or Petey, for that matter. But I think we need to find more clues. And open the door to some other suspects, too."

"I'm not a suspect though, right?" Teeny asked. "Buck was my favorite person in Pine Grove and I admired his originality."

Teeny smiled, proud of herself. Miss May and I laughed, but my laughter masked my unease. No, I didn't think Teeny had killed Buck...

...but I wasn't sure she could avoid looking or sounding guilty for much longer.

16

CABIN FEVER

One of the things that made Pine Grove great was that there was a wonderful supply of cute, affordable homes, all within walking distance of the town. Most people, when they moved to Pine Grove from New York City, like Hannah and Buck, insisted on procuring one of the houses closest to town. City transplants loved the idea of being able to walk everywhere, just like they could in the city. Plus, the houses surrounding Pine Grove's quaint downtown were each old, unique, and charming.

But unlike most city people, when Buck and Hannah moved up, they had not chosen one of those cute littles houses near town. Instead, they'd purchased a small log cabin down a gravel road all the way at the edge of the county line.

As I drove the pickup down the gravel road toward Buck and Hannah's cabin, Teeny and Miss May couldn't get over their disbelief at the remote location of the house. "I knew the guy was weird," said Teeny. "But this is extreme. I don't think anyone has lived in this cabin for over fifty years, at least."

"I know," said Miss May. "And this guy has to commute to *Peter's Land and Sea* every day. That must take him twenty minutes!"

"A twenty minute commute isn't that much for people coming from New York City. When I worked in the city running my interior design business, I would sometimes travel one or even two hours to go meet a client at their home. Buck and Hannah were probably delighted by only having to travel twenty minutes — especially because there's no traffic anywhere."

Teeny shook her head. "The city warps people's brains. They pay insane prices to live in tiny shoeboxes with no windows. They spend five hours a day going back and forth from work. And all just so they can make money? Up here you can make way less money, live in a bigger house, and have more free time to spend watching your favorite shows!"

"Don't say that too loud," said Miss May. "The people down in Manhattan will hear you."

Teeny shoved her head up into the front seat and looked over at me. "How did you find out where Buck and Hannah live again?"

"Liz told me. She interviewed them in their cabin for an article in the *Pine Grove Gazette* when they moved to town. I thought I remembered seeing a photo of the happy couple at their rustic home, and I was right."

"Nice job, Chels," said Teeny. "But do you think you can drive a little more gentle over this gravel? These bumps in the road are loosening my molar." Teeny reached her mouth and wiggled her tooth. "Or maybe it's always that loose. I should go to the dentist."

The log cabin was nestled in a dense patch of forest with a stone path leading from the front door, around a bend and over to the driveway. The three of us trekked up the path and around the corner. And that's when we saw Hannah, sitting on the porch steps, smoking a cigarette. She took a long, slow drag, then exhaled a cloud of smoke with a deep sigh.

Hannah looked over and watched as we approached. She didn't stand, nor did she wave, nor did she look happy to see us. Suddenly my stomach started doing somersaults. I'd forgotten how much I hated questioning the spouses of the deceased. Mourning the loss of a loved one was always difficult, and that difficulty was multiplied tenfold when the people in your town suspected you of murdering the person you were mourning.

Miss May stopped walking a few feet from Hannah, pressed her palms together and bowed her head. "Hannah. Hi. How are you? I'm so sorry for your loss."

Teeny and I murmured similar condolences.

Hannah breathed out another cloud of smoke. "I feel like I'm not in my body. Like I'm incapable of feeling anything my body typically feels. There's no hunger, no boredom, no curiosity. That's what I miss the most. The curiosity... The desire to learn anything new about the world. Everything feels so... empty." She looked up at us. "Have any of you ever lost your curiosity? Do you know how that feels?"

Miss May and Teeny stammered and muttered more condolences. Meanwhile, I flashed back to the year my parents died. Had I lost my curiosity then? I didn't think so.

I'd moved in with Miss May and started working on the farm — my aunt held the firm belief that hard work was a panacea. When I wasn't at the orchard, I'd been shuffled from one activity to another, from one class to another, from one grief counselor to another. I didn't remember feeling a lack of curiosity. All I remembered was loss. Like every day I woke up and realized anew the absence of the people I loved. I felt bad for Hannah, or anyone else, going through that.

I snapped back to the moment just in time to witness Miss May digging a pie from her purse and handing it to Hannah. Hannah accepted the pie and set it down on the steps beside her. "You fit that entire pie in your purse? Impressive."

"I'm the apple pie lady. It's required that my purse accommodates my title."

Hannah let out a small laugh, then Miss May pressed on in a gentle tone. "This must be so hard for you. I've never been married so I could never understand what it feels like to lose a spouse. And he was your coworker too. Everywhere you go, you must see reminders of Buck. I'm so sorry that all we can offer to help are words and pie."

Hannah took another long drag. "I'm not reminded of Buck as much as you might think." She ashed the cigarette in a little gold tray on her lap.

I looked over at Miss May with intrigue. *What was that supposed to mean?*

"How do you mean?" I asked Hannah.

"Nothing. Nevermind."

"You can talk to us," said Teeny in her most innocent voice. "Really. Tell us anything. We're vaults of secrecy, all three of us."

Hannah stubbed out the cigarette in the ashtray and stood up. "I don't need to talk. I'm fine. Everything is fine." Hannah cleared her throat and smoothed out her pants. "OK. Thank you for the apple pie. Sorry to rush you out like this but I just remembered I have a phone call with the funeral director. A lot of arrangements need to be made, you know? Thanks again."

Hannah hurried up the stairs toward the door. Miss May followed after Hannah as if to say something else, but my aunt was too slow.

Hannah closed the door in Miss May's face. Then she locked the deadbolt, and we could hear her footsteps thudding up the staircase to the second floor.

"That was weird," I said.

Miss May nodded. "We need to find out more."

17

FRIES AND LIES

*W*e stopped at *Ewing's Eats* for a quick bite on our way from Hannah's house back into town. *Ewing's* was a side-of-the-road burger spot with a legendary reputation and food to match. The proprietor, Patrick Ewing, was a great guy. And there were three little red tables in the parking lot that were perfect for grabbing a casual lunch.

When we arrived there was only one other car in the parking lot. It belonged to Rita, a barista at *The Brown Cow*. Rita was seated at one of the red tables, enjoying a burger and feeding the occasional French fry to her adorable toddler, Vinny Junior.

I'd first gotten to know Rita when she was one of the "mean girls" in my high school. But when I moved back to town I had gotten to know her better through our first murder investigation and I realized she had matured into a nice lady. Rita could be rough around the edges from time to time but she had a good heart. And her baby was cuter than a cartoon Cupid.

Rita was 100% Italian-American, with shiny, black hair

and captivating green eyes. Little Vinny looked just like her, with the same eyes and a big, pouty mouth. And the two of them smiled wide as they shared their junk food on that beautiful fall day.

Rita waved when she saw me, Teeny, and Miss May approaching from the parking lot.

"Chelsea. Ladies. How are you? Long time. Here for some guilty snacking? Me too. These curly fries are ridiculous. Here. Eat one, eat one."

Rita shoved her basket of fries toward me. "No one has ever had to force me to eat a French fry," I said. I grabbed a fry and popped it into my mouth. Teeny and Miss May did the same.

"Wow," said Teeny. "So good!"

"You should ask Patrick what his secret is," Miss May said. "I think he fries them in peanut oil and that makes them extra crispy. Something like that."

Teeny held up her hand. "Don't know. Don't care. I never need to know the magician's secrets. I just want to get sawed in half and put back together again so I can go home and have a nice night's sleep."

"How have you two been?" I asked Rita. "You look great." I squatted down and babbled at little Vinny. "And you are just the cutest most handsome little man in Pine Grove. You look like you're ready to put on a suit and tie and strut around your Manhattan office."

Rita rolled her eyes. "Don't put any ideas in his head. I want this kid close to home." She poked Vinny's perfect little nose. "You feel free to achieve greatness, baby. But if you're working in the city you're visiting your mother every weekend. Starting on Thursday night. And you're taking her to the Caribbean in December. That's non-negotiable."

Vinny made a little baby noise and Rita gave him a stern look. "You better believe I'm serious."

Rita popped a pacifier in Vinny's mouth and looked back over to us. "Unbelievable what happened with Buck over at *Peter's Land and Sea*. First that place explodes in popularity with all those fancy ingredients. Then the guy turns up dead. I heard he was in the basement or something? You three need to solve this one fast. I'm not in the mood to have a killer walking the streets. It's too stressful. But can I be honest? I think Buck's food was just OK. Did you try it? Gourmet ingredients but it didn't blow me away. Maybe those truffles were second-rate."

"Is there such a thing as a second-rate truffle?" I asked.

Rita shrugged. "There's a one to ten scale for everything. Even luxury items. You and me, we go on a yacht, it automatically seems nice and fancy 'cuz it's a yacht. But rich people go on a yacht, they see everything with a critical eye. The napkins aren't folded right. The windows have streaks on them. Every room is a little too hot or a little too cold or the sun is too bright. For rich people, a yacht can be a one. Truffles operate the exact same way. I'm pretty sure of it."

Teeny rubbed her chin. "You're right. I didn't think about it because Petey never charges us. But those truffle dishes were so inexpensive. At most places, if you had just a drop or two of truffle oil, that adds five, six dollars to the price. But I don't think they were doing that at *Peter's Land and Sea*."

"Interesting," said Miss May. "Maybe the restaurant wasn't doing as well as thought. Just because someplace is crowded doesn't mean it's making money."

I pointed at Miss May. "True. Amazon lost millions of dollars before it turned a single penny of profit, and that website was doing countless transactions every day."

"Listen to you, business girl," said Rita. "Knowing statistics about Amazon."

"I took a class in college," I said, sheepishly, "and I've listened to a few business podcasts. It's not that impressive."

"Yes it is," said Teeny. "Chelsea is very smart. It's annoying."

We all laughed, then Miss May took a step toward Rita and spoke in a softer voice. "Hey, let me ask you something... You're single, right?"

"Unfortunately, yes. Terminally single, if you know what I mean. Sorry. Dark humor. Not a ton of eligible bachelors in this area, though. And the ones that are here all like Chelsea."

"Oh, well..." I stammered, blushing and uncertain how to receive Rita's comment. "What were you saying Miss May?"

I wanted my aunt to bail me out of the awkward moment, but I also wondered about her line of questioning. *Why did she care about Rita's love life? Was Miss May moonlighting as an apple orchard-owning, mystery-solving, matchmaker on the side?*

"I know it's hard to find a guy," said Miss May. "But have you tried any of those apps? I've heard some success stories..."

"I'm so happy I didn't have to get on those apps to find Big Dan," said Teeny. "I don't come across well online. People need to see me and experience my charisma and beauty in person in order to love me. And I don't think Big Dan would go on an online dating site if his life depended on it."

"You're lucky, Teeny." Rita's shoulders slumped. "I've used all the sites. Every single one of them. One time I met a guy in Blue Mountain and he took me for a walk around some little dirty pond. But that's about the best date I've been on since Vinny was born."

"This might seem strange," said Miss May. "But did you ever see Buck on one of those dating sites?"

Rita tossed a few curly fries and her mouth and continued her mouth full. "Oh yeah. He hit me up constantly for a date. 'I love your eyes, girl.' 'I'll cook for you, sweetheart.' All that garbage. But I don't want a man with tattoos. I don't think tattoos are going to age well on anyone, personally."

"He was openly dating even though he was married ?" I asked.

Rita shook her head. "Not married. Separated. He explained the whole story to me in a message online. 'My wife and I can't make it work. We're separated. It's headed toward divorce. Blah blah blah.' It was all too complicated. Come to think of it, those complications were almost worse than the tattoos. And I like a man who can hold his own in the kitchen. Too bad."

Miss May, Teeny, and I exchanged knowing looks. Hannah had gotten weird back at the cabin. Had she almost slipped up and admitted she and Buck were on the outs?

Rita noticed our glances and subsequent silence and she cracked a big smile. "Oh boy! That was a clue, wasn't it? You didn't know about Hannah and Buck splitting up!" Rita raised both fists in the air with triumph. "I helped an investigation. I'm one of the sleuths! Heck, maybe I even solved the case." Rita leaned forward. "Do you think Hannah did it? She seems like a killer to me."

"I'm not sure what to think," said Miss May. "But I've got lots of questions and I need answers. Fast."

18

DINING AND DASHING

*W*e took our burgers to go and jumped back in my pickup.

I sped back toward town as the three of us discussed what to do next in our investigation. Rita's information about Buck and Hannah's separation was prime gossip. But more importantly, it was a breakthrough in the case. At least that's how it felt.

"Chelsea," said Miss May. "Slow down. You're going 50 in a 35!"

"Let the girl drive," said Teeny. "This could be a matter of life and death. Wait. Where are we going?"

I gripped the wheel so hard it made my forearms tired. "I don't know. But we're going there fast."

Teeny took a bite of her burger. "I like the way you think. Drive, Speed Racer. Drive."

"You two need to relax. Maybe we should go back to the farm and get my van so I can drive," said Miss May. "We need a plan. And a destination."

"I know," I said. "But I feel so pumped right now. Hannah and Buck were separated. She totally got weird when we were talking back at her house, and I bet it's because she was about to reveal the separation to us."

"I know," said Teeny. "She went on and on with that speech about grief and not feeling things and losing her curiosity. Meanwhile, she's not even with the guy anymore! And he's trolling around for young moms on the Internet. Not only is this a breakthrough in the case, it's an amazing source of protein for my gossip gremlin."

I glanced at Teeny in the rearview mirror. "Gossip gremlin?"

"Yep," said Teeny. "A gossip gremlin is a little gremlin that lives in your body and when you get a good piece of gossip, the gremlin eats it up."

"That's... super creepy," I said. "Does everyone have a gossip gremlin? Do I have one?"

"We all have gossip gremlins," said Miss May. "But you know what we don't have? A plan. And we're still lacking a destination."

"Let's go to the *Dragonfly Inn*," I said. The *Dragonfly Inn* was Pine Grove's only hotel and it just so happened to be owned and operated by Teeny's gruff sister, Peach. "I have a feeling Buck might have been staying there during his separation. And if he was staying there, maybe Peach can tell us if anything suspicious happened in the days before the murder."

"That's perfect," said Teeny. "Peach has my DVD box set of the fourth season of *Jenna and Mr. Flowers*. I want it back."

"Haven't you already seen it?" I asked.

"Yeah but I don't remember it," Teeny said. "So hurry up!"

We entered the lobby of the inn to find it completely empty. The phone was ringing. A small TV played an episode of *Father Brown* in the corner. And a steaming cup of coffee rested on the counter near Peach's chair.

Teeny looked around and gulped. "Peach isn't here. She might have been abducted. The killer who murdered Buck took my sister! Oh poor Peach! Why her? She was too young. I mean, not that young. Older than me. But still kind of young! And I have no idea where she put those DVDs. Now I'll never get them back!"

A grizzled smoker's voice rang out from the back room. "Calm down, Teeny. I'm right back here. Sometimes you are such a walking panic attack." Peach shuffled into the lobby holding a big bowl of cereal and eating it with a spoon. "I was just getting my midmorning snack. They say you need to eat six times a day to get skinny. I eat 10 times a day but it doesn't seem to be helping."

Peach settled into her chair with a groan. She was heftier than Teeny, wearing jeans and an oversized cat sweater. But she had Teeny's sparkling blue eyes and mischievous energy.

Teeny crossed her arms "I am not a walking panic attack."

"Yes you are. And you were more concerned about your *Mr. Flowers* box set than you were about your dearly departed sister. Don't bother to apologize. Just tell me what you need. Do I have another cold-blooded murderer staying at my fine establishment? At this point, I should start offering discounts for killers. One night free for every person you kill. How does that sound?"

"Sounds depressing and grim," said Miss May. "And like it encourages the wrong kind of behavior."

Peach snorted. "Take a joke, Mabel."

"We're not here looking for a murderer," I said. "We were actually wondering... Was that chef, Buck, staying here?"

Peach slapped her palm to her forehead. "Of course. That makes more sense. I forgot that guy had even stayed here. I would offer a discount to murder victims too, but there's little chance they're going to be repeat customers. Get it, Mabel? Because they're dead."

Miss May gave Peach a tight smile. "I get it, Peach. Good one. Ha. Ha."

Peach gathered a few keys off the pegboard behind her and came around to our side of the counter. "You're going to have to be patient because I forget which room he was in."

"The police haven't been here to check it out?" asked Miss May, casting a sidelong glance in my direction.

"You know the cops in this town," said Peach. "Chelsea knows them better than any of us."

"What's that supposed to mean?" I asked.

"Nothing, sweetheart. I'm just saying. These cops talk a lot of talk but they don't do much of anything. Follow me."

Peach groaned as she walked up the steps, one foot at a time. "This Buck guy has been staying here for a couple months now. He was one of my long term crashers. I guess he and his lady were splitting up."

"Everyone had that information but us," said Miss May. "I'm beginning to worry we're becoming less connected to the rumor mill."

"If Chelsea would start online dating she would know about every single man in town," said Teeny. "But she just has to have a boyfriend. And a handsome detective on deck."

"Sorry," I said. "I'll try to be less romantically successful."

"Don't apologize to these two for anything," said Peach as she reached the second floor. "They can online date if they want. You don't have to do anything they say. You do you."

Peach paused to catch her breath when we reached the second floor. Then she started opening random doors to try to find Buck's accommodations. The first door she opened introduced us to an old man who was using the toilet. The second room led us to a maid who was napping in an unmade guest bed. The third room was empty.

Finally, we came to the last room at the end of the hall. Peach popped open the door and nodded. "Yup. This is the one. Have fun."

Peach stepped aside and we entered. And I was immediately shocked by what I saw inside.

19

CLEAN YOUR ROOM!

*B*uck's room was so messy it was hard to believe only one man had been staying there.

Piles of clothes obscured every inch of the floor. Fast food wrappers were scattered on every surface, which surprised me considering Buck's reputation as a gastronomical wunderkind. And the bathroom sink was caked in dried toothpaste and beard trimmings.

The room looked as though someone had locked a trio of teenage boys inside and said, "Figure it out."

Miss May kicked at a pile of dirty clothes with her loafer. "I can't believe this place. Buck had a tidy appearance. He seemed so concerned with how he looked, what with the tattoos and his carefully groomed little beard. But this place is horrifying."

Teeny turned to Peach. "Are you sure this is the right room?"

I pointed at the floor where a few chefs whites were crumpled up and stained. "Those are his clothes. You can see the *Peter's Land and Sea* logo on that shirt."

"How are we going to find a clue in this mess?" asked Teeny.

"Maybe this mess is a clue," I said. "Maybe Buck was mentally unstable or perhaps he had a secret teenage son... Or three."

"I suppose," Miss May said. "But I don't understand. Peach, doesn't the maid service at the *Dragonfly* clean every day?"

"When they're not napping, they're supposed to be cleaning," said Peach. "But Buck requested no maid service for his stay. Negotiated a lower room rate for it. Said he didn't want anybody prying around. Maybe he was embarrassed by his insane sloppiness."

"The guy was disgusting," said Teeny. Then she clapped a hand over her mouth. "Whoops. I forgot my new rules. Let's see... Buck was so clean. And he wasn't a sicko at all. He seems like he was a great guy and I don't understand why Hannah didn't want to be with him anymore."

"We don't know that Hannah left him," I said. "It's possible Buck left her. Although this room does seem like it was home to someone who lost the will to clean from heartbreak and depression."

"Did Buck do anything suspicious while he was here, Peach?" Miss May asked.

"Pretty suspicious to request no maid. Beyond that... He drank a lot of coffee every morning. He had a couple of angry phone calls in the lobby. I assumed those conversations were between the exiled slob and his wife. I don't know. I'm suspicious of anyone with more than one tattoo. He had an entire arm covered so I looked at him funny everywhere he went."

"You're such a good host," said Miss May.

"Buzz off. The guy was clearly a demented sicko. I was right to make him feel like one."

I crossed over to the TV stand. Several bottles of water were clustered around the TV, alongside a few empty cans and an extra large energy drink. The energy drink stuck to the wood when I tried to pull it up and left a large ring on the wooden surface.

Peach shook her head. "See? Who does that? Demented."

"How do you suggest we proceed?" I asked Miss May.

Miss May looked around with her hands on her hips. "I guess we need to go through this stuff."

I looked at the mess and squinted like I was peering directly into the sun. "OK then. Let's get started."

For the next couple hours, the three of us sorted through Buck's collection of filth with great care. Miss May checked the pockets of every article of clothing on the floor and found nothing more than empty gum wrappers, bottle caps, and rubber bands.

Teeny handled the clothes that remained in the closet. She found a grocery list that consisted only of gourmet items, truffles chief among them. But she didn't find anything else of note.

I handled the surfaces, including the coffee table, the TV stand, the dresser, and, *ew*, the bathroom.

Most of the surfaces were cluttered with sticky bottles like the one I'd pried off the TV stand. I also had the unfortunate luck to find a pile of stinky socks on one of the nightstands alongside a deposit of crusty old tissues. But I had a breakthrough just a few minutes after I began investigating the bathroom. There, resting on the back of the toilet, was a hairbrush matted with tangled, long, brown hair.

I grabbed the hairbrush and rushed into the bedroom. "Look. I found something."

Teeny shrugged. "It's a hairbrush. So what?"

"Oh my goodness!" Miss May stepped forward and took the hairbrush from me like she was handling live dynamite.

"What is it, May?" Teeny squealed.

Miss May swallowed hard. "Buck was bald. And his wife... is a blonde."

20

I SCREAM, YOU SCREAM, EXTRA
SPRINKLES PLEASE

*M*iss May, Teeny and I went straight from the *Dragonfly* to Pine Grove's newest ice cream shop to discuss our recent discovery. The place was called *Cherry on Top*. It was housed in a cute white building. And the owner, Emily, was just as cute.

Emily greeted us with a big smile. "Hey! How are you three doing? Stressed from the recent investigation and looking for a creamy pick-me-up?"

"You know me too well, Emily," said Teeny. "You're like my bartender and my therapist and my priest all rolled up into one."

"One scoop vanilla, one scoop chocolate, rainbow sprinkles, chocolate sprinkles, sprinkles on the side?"

Teeny smiled wide. "Make it a double."

Miss May and I followed Teeny and placed our orders with enthusiasm. I got a kid's cone of Moose Tracks and Miss May got an ice cream sundae with graham crackers and honey.

Emily chatted with us as she prepared our treats. "Any big breakthroughs in the case? I'm here to help if you need me. I always keep one ear to the ground. Hurts my neck sometimes, but I like to be informed."

Miss May shifted her weight from one foot to the other. "We have a couple of decent ideas but nothing concrete. Keep your eyes peeled for us."

"Like I said, my ear is always to the ground." Emily pointed to a trio of security cameras posted near the entrance. "And my cameras are always on."

Emily served us our ice cream with a big grin. "These are on the house, ladies. You three do a great service for this town. You deserve a free treat once in a while."

Miss May demurred. "Please let us pay."

She held out some cash but Emily pushed her hand away. "I said it's on the house! Don't insult me."

"Fine," said Miss May. "But you can't reject this tip." With lightning speed, Miss May jammed a $10 bill into the tip jar. Emily laughed and crossed her arms.

Miss May returned the laugh with a shrug. "I've been doing this for a long time, sweetheart. You've got to be faster than that."

We chose a table off to the side of the ice cream shop where no one on Main Street could hear us talk, then we dug into our treats and our conversation with equal ferocity.

"So what are we thinking about this suspicious hairbrush?" Miss May asked.

Teeny wiggled in her seat. "Oh. OK. I have a theory."

"Your theory won't count if it's from *Jenna and Mr. Flowers*," said Miss May.

"But it's pertinent," said Teeny. "Is that the right word? Pertinent?"

"We won't know until you share your theory," I said.

"OK. So in a recent episode of *Jenna and Mr. Flowers*—"

"Knew it," said Miss May.

"Can I talk?" asked Teeny.

"Sorry."

"OK. So. I think it was season seven, episode thirty-eight... Mr. Flowers started wearing a wig all over town so nobody would know who he was. And the whole mystery was tied up in his 'secret identity.'"

"So you think Buck had been wearing a wig around Pine Grove?" I asked.

"That's right," said Teeny. "I think Buck had been wearing a brown wig around town for months, sneaking through the shadows like a totally different person. And he was using that hairbrush on the wig. If that were true, Buck may have been in all sorts of places we haven't been looking for him. 'Cuz he was in disguise!"

"I think it would be hard for someone with those kind of tattoos to hide in plain sight," said Miss May. "But I suppose it could have been strands of Buck's wig in the hairbrush."

"People don't brush wigs, I don't think," I said. "Besides, I didn't see a wig in that pig sty of a room. Did either of you see one?"

Miss May and Teeny shook their heads. No wig had been discovered, brown, purple, blue, or otherwise.

"If the long, brown hair didn't come from a wig," said Miss May, "I think it came from the head of a woman."

Teeny widened her eyes. "The head of a dead woman? So you think Buck was a killer too. That sneaky, conniving, ugly—"

"I don't think Buck was a killer," said Miss May. "I think the hair in the brush belonged to a living woman. Like maybe someone with whom Buck was having an affair?"

Teeny gasped. "That's a good theory!"

"But you think this relationship with the brown-haired woman caused the separation from Hannah?" I asked. "Or do you think Buck's relationship with the brown-haired woman came after he moved out on his own?"

"I think they separated because Hannah found out about the cheating," said Teeny. "Infidelity causes marital problems all the time. It's probably the number one cause of divorce. Either that or arguing about what shows to watch."

"True," I said. "Plus it's hard for me to imagine that Buck found a new partner while he was living out of a filthy hotel room. No man could get a woman with such a dirty abode. So I think Buck and this mystery woman were involved before the separation, and I think they had been together since Buck was living with Hannah in a nice house. The brown-haired woman probably had no idea what a slob Buck was until he moved out of the house he shared with Hannah."

"Maybe the brown-haired woman killed him once she realized how gross he was," said Teeny. "Like, she was so disgusted that she'd had an affair with such a slovenly crea-ture that she had to murder him. That wouldn't shock me."

"That's not a strong motive for murder," Miss May said.

Teeny pouted. "Then what do you think is up with the brown-haired woman? How do you think she's connected to this case?"

Miss May shrugged. "I don't know. But this feels important."

"Do either of you have any ideas about who the woman might be?" I asked.

Miss May and Teeny shrugged. Then I looked up and down Main Street for a clue. I saw several brown-haired women out and about in town. Pine Grove was having a great hair day. But one of those women might have been wrapped up in something very, very bad.

21

TO DYE FOR

*T*eeny needed to go back to her restaurant after ice cream so I dropped her off, and Miss May and I headed back to the farm. It was late afternoon and the sun was beginning to set across Pine Grove. The hills behind town jumped with vibrant reds, yellows and oranges. The whole scene was peaceful and serene.

I was eager to discuss the possible identity of the brown haired woman. But Miss May spent the drive making phone calls to handle orchard business.

First, my aunt called the facility that bottled and labeled our homemade apple cider. It was a family-run factory a couple of hours away in New Jersey. The old Italian man on the other end of the line sounded tough. But Miss May managed to reduce our cost per finished good by a few cents. That didn't seem like a lot, but she later explained to me that those few cents applied across every bottle would earn the farm thousands of dollars a year.

Miss May was still on the phone when we arrived home so I was left with a good deal of what I like to call, "Chelsea time."

I whistled for Steve the dog and he came running on his three good legs and one limpy leg out of the farmhouse to greet me. Then the two of us walked the grounds of the orchard. I took Steve along my favorite route, tracing the brook on the outer edge of the property. It had rained in the last week so the brook moved with extra energy. Steve splashed around like a little kid (or I guess, like a dog), and I snapped a few pictures of him on my phone. *You can never have too many pictures of your fur babies, am I right?*

We ran into KP out among the apple trees. KP was Miss May's right hand man on the farm, a jack-of-all-trades who helped with maintenance, finances, and sometimes even cooking. He had a gruff exterior but a soft heart, and he was surprisingly fond of Steve and the other animals on the farm.

The moment we came across KP, he was wearing sweatpants and a sweatshirt with sweat bands over his wrists and forehead, pumping his legs and walking in place. I giggled. "KP. Hi. Are you out here getting ripped?"

KP scoffed. "No way. I was in great shape for my whole 20's. Overrated, if you ask me. If you're too lean, you've got nowhere to rest the clicker while you're watching TV. I'm just trying to get out here and get moving. I saw a segment on *Good Morning America* about the importance of moving your body. Keeps your mind sharp too. You know about all that, right?"

"Everybody's exercising lately. Miss May walked all the way to *Grandma's* from the farm."

KP widened his eyes. "Had no idea that old bird could still fly. Good for her. I bet you beat her there by a mile."

"I woke up late and drove."

KP chuckled. "Like I said. Bet you beat her there."

"Actually, no. She still got there before me," I said. "I woke up very late."

KP and I laughed. He leaned over and gave Steve a pet. "This guy's getting scruffy. He needs some TLC. Better call the groomer before people start thinking he's a stray."

"I agree. Even the tramp from *Lady and the Tramp* had a better haircut than this. I'll find a groomer to come up and take care of it."

KP resumed pumping his legs and added a strange little twist to his movements, which I suspected was for my amusement. "Have a nice walk."

I smiled. "Thanks. Have a nice... Whatever this is."

Steve and I strolled through the orchard for another hour or two. When we got home, Miss May was setting the table and there was a fresh, hot pizza on the counter.

I thrust both my fists in the air. "Pizza party mystery detective time."

Miss May shook her head. "You are so much the same as when you were a kid. I knew pizza would make you happy. Grab a slice. I've been thinking."

I opened the box. Inside there was a square pizza with fresh slices of mozzarella and plenty of dark red sauce and fresh basil. In New York, we call this a "grandma pie." It's thin and crispy and so light and fresh even a grandma could finish the whole thing by herself. *Not sure if that's where the name comes from, but I like to think so.*

I slid a slice onto my plate and the cheese stretched and bubbled. When I took a bite, I let out a soft sigh and slumped down in my chair. "I had no idea I was even hungry, but now I realize I was starving." I took another big bite. "So how are we going to figure out whose hair was on that brush?"

"You tell me," said Miss May.

"I mean, there's so many brown-haired women in town. Could be anyone."

"But let's work with the clues we have," said Miss May.

"Then I guess I would point to Rebecca."

"Why?" Miss May leaned forward.

"Because… Because Rebecca showed up at the out-of-order bathroom at the exact time Buck was supposed to be there? I don't think that was a coincidence. I think it was a romantic rendezvous or maybe it was a romantic rendezvous gone wrong."

"Interesting."

"But there's one important detail that doesn't add up…"

"Rebecca has red hair."

I took my last bite of pizza and nodded with my mouth full. "Exactly."

"Hair colors can change," Miss May pointed out. "You had blue hair when you were seventeen. But somehow it made its way back to beautiful dirty blonde."

"Let's not attack my blue hair," I said. "I think it was a good look. But I see your point. Rebecca could have dyed her hair red, or brown, or any color. At any point."

Miss May nodded. "I'll call Petey and ask about Rebecca's hair."

I nodded. "I'll have another slice of pizza while I wait."

Petey picked up on the first ring. Miss May exchanged quick pleasantries then got down to business.

"I wanna ask you something about your waitress, Rebecca."

Miss May put Petey on speaker so I could here.

"OK. Anything," Petey said through the phone.

"Right now her hair is red. Has it always been red?"

"Yeah." Peter answered in an instant. "She's the red-haired waitress. For sure."

Miss May looked over at me with narrowed eyes. "So Rebecca's hair has always been red. You think she's a natural redhead, not someone who dyed it that color?"

"I think so," Petey said. "Her eyebrows are red too. And she has freckles."

"Petey..." I began, "how many waitresses do you have there?"

"Oh hey, Chelsea," Petey said. "Honestly, I don't even know. Too many. Buck had some crazy system where every waitress should only work three hour shifts. So we had to hire a lot of girls and shuffle them around constantly. Scheduling was a disaster."

"Did you only hire girls?" I asked.

"I've got a couple guys on staff from when I opened this place. But yeah, Buck insisted we hire female servers. He said women are gentler and more graceful than men... Less likely to spill. Something like that. I've got to have at least thirty or forty women on staff. A gaggle of girls from every surrounding town."

Miss May rested her chin in her hand. "Is it possible you don't know the hair color of every waitress? Or that if one of your servers dyed her hair, you might not notice?"

"Oh," said Petey. "Yeah. I guess it's possible. I feel so confident because I've seen so much of Rebecca lately... Because of this whole Buck situation. But to be honest, I don't totally remember when I hired her or what she looked like then. Not even sure if I interviewed her at all."

Miss May sighed. "OK, Petey. Thanks for chatting with us. Get back to your night."

Miss May glanced at me, looking a little hopeless.

"Don't worry," I said. "I have a better idea. But it will have to wait until tomorrow."

Miss May took a big bite of pizza and looked at me like, *this better be good.*

Miss May and I showed up at Jennifer Paul's hair salon first thing the next morning. Jennifer had been on quite the emotional and spiritual journey since I had arrived in Pine Grove. First, she had struggled with her mental health, rather publicly. Then she'd briefly converted her hair salon to a yoga studio. Finally, she'd added hair care back to the yoga studio and settled on a combination of the two businesses. According to local gossip she had finally found stability and balance and I was excited to see her that morning.

Jennifer gave us a perky greeting as we walked up. "Hey, ladies! Haircuts, yoga, murder suspect, or all three?"

"None of the above," I said. "Quick question for you."

"I didn't do it. I wasn't in town the night Buck was killed. And I've been taking my meds."

I put my hands up to show my neutrality. "We don't suspect you of murder. Really." I pulled out my smart phone and opened to a picture of Rebecca that I had found on the Internet. She was smiling, on a hike, with red hair. "But do you know this girl?"

"Rebecca. Yep."

"And have you ever colored her hair?" I asked.

22

HAIR DIED

"You were right!" Miss May started talking as soon as we shut the doors of the pickup and clicked in our seat belts. "Jennifer dyed Rebecca's hair red last week. And before that it was long and brown. Just like the hair in the hairbrush! Good job, Chelsea. You were right. Jennifer had the info."

"So you think Buck and Rebecca were definitely having an affair?"

Miss May took a deep breath through her nostrils. "Definitely is a strong word. But I suspect it now more than ever."

I started the car and drove away. "Agreed. But the hair on the brush was brown, not red... So if Rebecca had her hair dyed red a week ago that means she hadn't been with Buck for at least a week."

"Maybe they had a falling out before Rebecca dyed her hair," Miss May suggested. "Maybe they had begun to hate each other and when they saw one another at work, it filled both of them with fury."

"Or maybe the hair on the brush belonged to another

brown-haired girl," I said. "Sounds like Buck was quite the creep, hiring only women at the restaurant."

"That is an old-fashioned misogynistic policy," said Miss May. "But I don't want to get distracted with the idea of other women just yet. Let's try to stay focused and confirm the affair. If we can find out whether or not Buck had a relationship with Rebecca, that could be a big deal for this investigation."

I took a hard left turn. "I'll head to *Peter's Land and Sea*."

"Not today," said Miss May. "Pull a U-turn. *Land and Sea* caters a big lunch every Wednesday for the retirees at *Washington Villages*. If you drive to the villages now, we'll arrive just in time for the food to be served."

I checked the clock. "It's barely 11 AM."

"That's lunch time for old folks."

I pulled a U-turn and headed for the villages. Many of our prior investigations had taken us to *Washington Villages*, mostly because the older residents there loved gossip and had all sorts of helpful information. Also because, occasionally, one or two of the residents were suspects in our investigations. But each visit had been exciting and suspenseful. As we pulled up, a warm nostalgic feeling flooded my body. Maybe it's odd to have nostalgia for prior murder investigations, but what can I say? The human heart is a complicated thing.

Washington Villages was a classy retirement community with big, columned white buildings, two tennis courts and plenty of green space.

Miss May circumvented the security check-in by walking around to the back of the building and we followed the *Land and Sea* catering staff inside the cafeteria.

Miss May and I huddled together in the corner of the large room to remain unseen as we devised our plan.

"Teeny is going to be so mad she missed this." I said as I scanned the crowd for Rebecca. "She loves to sneak. We should have called her."

"I texted her from the car. You didn't see that?"

"I guess not. Is she coming?"

Miss May shrugged. "No reply. But it might be better for the two of us to handle this on our own, anyway. We need to be quiet and stealthy. Not that Teeny isn't quiet and stealthy... But she's not."

I looked back out at the cafeteria. The catering staff had set up about twenty big, circular tables. Each table seated a handful of happy, elderly residents. I watched an ancient woman drink an entire mimosa in a single sip. I admired the white tablecloths and fancy dishware. And I reflected on how the team from *Land and Sea* had transformed the cafeteria into what felt like a nice restaurant without much effort.

I also couldn't help but notice all the cute, young waitresses bustling from table to table. "So many attractive young women at this event," I said.

"Yup," said Miss May. "But I don't see Rebecca anywhere."

"Me neither."

Miss May shook her head. "I suppose we should have seen this coming. Petey said he has several hundred million waitresses on staff and he schedules them in weird intervals, so I'm sure there are a bunch of them who aren't here today, not just Rebecca."

A loud crash rang out from across the room followed by a thud. I looked over and there stood Teeny, hands over her mouth, standing above an entire turkey that had been knocked to the floor. "Oh! I'm so sorry. I didn't see you there. Or the turkey."

Teeny was standing with an employee of *Washington Villages*, almost like she was on some kind of orientation tour. I marveled at her ability to make herself known so quickly upon entering.

"See?" Teeny said to her bewildered tour guide. "I told you I need this old folks' home. I can barely take care of myself. Everywhere I go, I'm running into turkeys."

"All of our residents can take care of themselves, miss. At *Washington Villages*, we merely provide a fun, social environment meant for active older individuals to enjoy life to the finest in their golden years."

"Great, great," said Teeny. "I think I see one of those fine golden-aged individuals across the room. That's my friend Miss May. I'm going to go say hi to her."

Miss May laughed. "Hi, Teeny. I can hear you."

Teeny edged past one of the circular tables as she approached us. "I can't believe the two of you were going to come on this mission without me."

"I texted you."

"You're supposed to call me. I never read my texts. Writing's too small. Don't know how to make it bigger."

"Why don't you wear your glasses?" I asked.

"I don't need glasses," Teeny said, frowning.

"But you can't read small print."

"My eyes are great," Teeny said. "Anyway, I got Siri or whoever that woman in my phone is to read my texts to me this morning. Lucky for you two. So now, voila, here I am!"

"Quite an entrance you made. How did you manage to knock over an entire turkey?" I asked.

"Oh, that turkey should have watched where it was going," Teeny said. "Not my fault. So what's the plan?"

Miss May shrugged. "I don't know for sure. We were trying to keep a low profile. Until you got here."

Someone cleared their throat from behind us. "I saw you standing here the whole time. You weren't hiding from me."

I turned to find our favorite *Washington Villages* resident, Petunia, smiling up at us from her seat at a banquet table.

"When you three need to do an investigation at *Washington Villages*, you're supposed to come straight to me. I've proven myself. Have I not proven myself?"

"Of course you've proven yourself, Petunia," said Miss May. "But—"

"But we didn't want to offend you," I said. "Sometimes when we show up here, you think we're accusing you of murder."

Petunia dismissed me with a snort, then grabbed my arm with the grip strength only older women have. "What's going on with your love life, Chelsea? Are you still with the lion tamer or have you wised up?"

"Lion tamer," I said.

Petunia clucked her tongue. "I have access to dozens of eligible grandsons, you know. Just say the word and I'll have you going on dates every night for ten years straight. A lot of these kids are weird, don't get me wrong. They've got twelve jobs driving people around and walking dogs, and all the while they say they're artists, that kind of thing. But you're weird too, so maybe you'd get along. What's up with this investigation?"

"I was trying to tell you," said Miss May. "We're not here to talk to any of the residents. "

"You're here to snoop on somebody who works at the *Villages*? Or to get information from one of these caterers?"

Miss May nodded. "The caterers. Yes."

"I can help with that, too," said Petunia. "For a price."

23

A HAIRY SITUATION

"Y ou're going to charge to help us with an investigation?" asked Teeny. "That's messed up. We're trying to find a killer here, Petunia. Don't stand in the way of justice. What if someone else gets killed while you're negotiating your fee? Then that blood is on your hands."

Petunia shrugged. "I provide a valuable service as an informant, and my mother always taught me to demand what I want in life. Besides, I've been losing at the poker tables for a month straight and I need a bigger bankroll. Are you really moving to *Washington Villages*, Teeny? I hope not. No offense, but you're kind of annoying."

Teeny gasped. "I am not annoying. People love me. Right?"

"Mixed reviews," said Miss May.

"Hey!"

"Relax, Teeny." I chuckled. "We love you a whole big bunch. Everyone does. Right, Petunia?"

"Eh. I still think you're annoying," said Petunia. "Now pay up."

"How do we know you're not going to make up some fictional clue to get your money?" Teeny asked. "Sounds like you're desperate for cash."

"That's an insult to my limited integrity," said Petunia. "I've never led you astray. And the three of you have accused me of murder more than once. Still. I tell you the truth, the whole truth, and nothing but the truth, so help me God. Ask my grandkids. They call me Honest Abe. Kind of an insulting moniker. I don't think I look like an Abe. But hey, they're kids, and kids are all stupid."

"Do your grandkids know their granny has a gambling problem?" Teeny asked.

"That's it," said Petunia. "I'm out. Forget it."

Miss May glared at Teeny. Teeny sighed. "OK. I'm sorry. I don't think you have a gambling problem. I just got fired up. Sometimes I start thinking like I'm in one of my TV shows and I get to talking like some wisecracking Brit."

Petunia narrowed her eyes. "What are your shows?"

"Lately it's been all *Jenna and Mr. Flowers*," said Teeny.

Petunia smiled so big it went from one ear all the way out the side of her head. It was the biggest smile that had ever crossed her face, at least in my presence, and it was adorable. "I love *Jenna and Mr. Flowers*. Mr. Flowers is always two steps ahead of the criminal and Jenna is such a good sidekick. She's hysterical. Sometimes she puts her foot in her mouth but you know she means well."

"That's like me," said Teeny. "And Chelsea, frankly. This girl has her foot in the mouth so much she might as well get foot-flavored toothpaste."

I crinkled my nose in disgust. But I couldn't disagree.

Petunia slapped her knee. "Foot-flavored toothpaste. Now I get it. You're the tough, funny one. You're spunky."

"That's right. Just like you," said Teeny.

"Listen," said Petunia. "I'm going to help you girls out for free today. Because I like you and I feel bad about the whole calling you annoying thing. But I want you know, it's the last time. From now on I'm going to need twenty bucks for every tip I provide. That's fair, right?

"Of course," said Miss May. "And I'll give you free pie anytime you're up at the orchard."

"I like the apple cider donuts. Chocolate covered."

"Those are my favorite too," said Teeny.

"Deal," said Miss May. "Free apple cider donuts, chocolate-covered, whenever you're up at the orchard. And I'll send you a box to your apartment every so often so you have something to snack on while you're watching your shows."

Petunia smiled again. "Donuts and mysteries. That's a good night. Throw in a little poker and I'm in heaven."

"Sorry to hear you've been losing," I said. "I'm sure it's just a bad run of cards."

Petunia shook her head. "I wish. It's Ethel. That old skeleton finally started betting real money at the table! Don't know where she got it. Probably finally tapped those stocks and bonds from the 50s. At first, it was like Christmas every day. Then she got good at bluffing!"

A tiny, much older woman leaned forward. It was Ethel. She cupped her hand around her ear. "What?"

Petunia yelled so Ethel could hear. "I said you've gotten good at bluffing."

"That's right," said Ethel. "You never know if I've got aces or deuces!"

Moments later, we were all seated around a little table beside a pond on the *Washington Villages* grounds. Miss May filled Petunia in on the case and concluded by asking Petunia if she knew anything about Rebecca and Buck.

"Oh yeah. Rebecca and Buck were involved," said Petunia. "Do you know what I mean by involved? I don't want to get dirty."

"We know what you mean," said Miss May in a rush.

"How do you know they were...together?" I asked Petunia. I wasn't eager for any sordid details, but I was curious about her source.

"I walked in on them in a storage closet. And let me tell you, they were really—"

"We get it," said Miss May, once again in a hurry. "What were you doing in the storage closet?"

"Stealing toilet paper. Only idiots pay for toilet paper in this community." Petunia took a big sip from a water bottle. "You probably want to know how I knew it was Rebecca, too. With all these pretty girls running around, an old lady like me might get confused."

"No one called you old," said Miss May.

"You didn't have to. I am old. And the reason I know it was Rebecca is because that minx was supposed to marry my grandson. Yep. Five years ago. They were engaged, and then she cheated on him."

"I thought your grandson was overseas in the military," said Miss May.

"He has been ever since he got his heart broken by that human pied-à-terre. Now he only comes home at Christmas. The girl crushed his spirit. Makes me so mad that she's still out there, running around with married men."

"Do you think Buck's wife knew about the affair?" asked Teeny.

Petunia shook her head. "Doubt it."

"When did you see them together?" Miss May inquired. "Any idea how long this is been going on?"

"I saw them two, maybe three weeks ago. But I didn't exactly revisit the storage closet when the caterers were here in the weeks after that, you know what I mean? I don't need to see that. It was graphic. I'm telling you, they were—"

"We get it," Teeny, Miss May, and I said at the same time.

"Let's just say it seemed to me that the two of them knew each other very well. Like it had been going on for a long time," Petunia said. "Probably would've gone on forever if the poor guy didn't go and get himself killed."

"Do you think Rebecca killed him?" Teeny asked.

Petunia looked Teeny square in the eye. "What do you think?"

24

WORKED TO THE BONE

*O*nce we left *Washington Villages* we decided to head back to *Peter's Land and Sea* to look around. Miss May argued that *Land and Sea* was most likely the nexus of Buck and Rebecca's affairs. She thought we might be able to take advantage of the empty restaurant, while everyone was at the catering event, to sneak inside and find a clue that might incriminate, or exonerate, Rebecca.

I suggested that we skip *Land and Sea* and go back to Rebecca's for straight talk. But Miss May pointed out that Rebecca was preoccupied, rude and clearly closed off. She also pointed out that Rebecca might have seen us run away with a bag of her trash, and she concluded that if we were to question Rebecca a second time, it would be best to have evidence more concrete than mis-matching hair in a brush.

We expected *Land and Sea* to be vacant when we arrived. But when we pulled up, there was another car in the parking lot. And it looked familiar to me.

"I think that's Hannah's car," I said. "But her husband just died. Why would she be at work?"

"People often throw themselves into their work instead

of grieving loss in an open and vulnerable way," said Teeny. "That's what I do too. I've never baked more in my life than when *Northport Diaries* got cancelled. That style of grieving is pretty common, I think. I heard all about it on *60 Minutes*."

"Now I feel even worse for Hannah," I said.

Miss May shrugged. "It's also possible she killed Buck in cold blood and came to the restaurant this afternoon to destroy evidence. Or maybe she's here because she feels totally normal and she doesn't care that Buck's gone."

"Hmm," I said. "On a scale of 'ice cold' to 'nervous sweats,' I wonder where the temperature of Hannah's heart falls."

"Regardless of her internal emotional thermometer, Hannah's a suspect. So don't pity her 'til she's proven inno-cent," Miss May said. "Plus, right now she's in our way. How are we going to snoop around that restaurant with Hannah inside?"

Teeny smiled. "I have an idea."

I groaned. Teeny's ideas usually involved shoving me into a window or twisting me into an otherwise uncomfort-able position. Fortunately, that day, her idea was less involved.

"I'm going to knock on the front door and make a big, stinking' scene about something," said Teeny. "May, you're going to help. When Hannah comes to the door we'll start screaming like crazy people. Meanwhile, Chelsea, you sneak around the back. While Hannah is out here dealing with us two lunatic ladies, you'll be inside the restaurant being a detective so hard it hurts."

"I don't know if that's—" I started.

But before I could get my sentence out, Teeny leapt out

of my truck, hurried to the restaurant and started banging on the front door.

"I sprained my ankle and I'm suing!" She yelled at the top of her lungs, which was still not that loud, then she looked over at me with a smirk. "I'm suing this restaurant for every last penny!"

Miss May nudged me. "You better get going."

I sighed, hopped out of the truck and hurried toward the back of the restaurant. Behind me, I heard Teeny continuing to belt out threats at the top of her tiny little lungs. "Your sidewalk is cracked and dangerous. This is an abomination!"

I took one last look as Miss May joined Teeny at the entrance to *Land and Sea*. Then I disappeared around the back.

The back door to the restaurant was open so I slipped inside without making a sound. I found myself in the dining room. The tables were half set. The lights were off. And I could hear quiet music in the distance. I followed the sound of the music toward the back office.

I stopped near the edge of the dining room to peak toward the front door. Hannah was up there arguing with Teeny about the state of the restaurant's sidewalks. But I knew the distraction couldn't last long. So I slipped into the office and resolved to work quick.

It was a small room with a few filing cabinets and a desk against the far wall. A computer was on the desk, along with a reservation notebook.

I looked down at the reservation book and deduced that Hannah had gone into the restaurant that morning to confirm weekend reservations. She had inserted comments on many of the reservations, like "needs a booster seat," or, "requests vegetarian," and had marked quite a few appointments as "cancelled."

I exited the office and spotted an employee break room across the hall. I tip-toed inside the room and made my way over to a wall of employee lockers. Sadly, there was a padlock on every door. I tugged on one of the padlocks and sighed. There was no way I was getting into those lockers.

"Two million dollars," I heard Teeny yell from out front.

"That's ridiculous," said Hannah. "You're wasting my time. Get out of this restaurant!"

"I'm not even in the restaurant, I'm on the front steps. And now it's three million."

I winced. Teeny's lie was going off the rails. That meant Hannah would be back in the office area soon. I hurried out of the break room and back over to the office computer. Maybe I could find a clue on there...

The computer woke up with a chime as soon as I moved the mouse and I began to investigate. The digital desktop was cluttered with random photos and documents, nothing strange there. But then I noticed that Microsoft Word had been minimized in the corner of the screen. I wondered why a restaurant would be using word processing software so I enlarged the window. It was a blank document with nothing but a blinking cursor.

Weird.

The arguing between Hannah and Teeny reached a crescendo at the front door. But I maintained focused on the document. Something felt off there.

I found the button for "Undo" and pressed it. Suddenly, as if by magic, a large chunk of text appeared on the screen. Someone must have typed the words and then deleted them. I enlarged the font and read it out loud in a soft whisper.

"*Peter's Land and Sea* seeks head chef. Gourmet restaurant or New York City experience preferred. Please contact Peter@PetersLandandSea.com. Salary negotiable."

I reread the message a couple of times and then I noticed an important detail... Peter's ad for a new head chef was dated Thursday, October 8... Two full days before Buck had been murdered.

Petey had told me and Miss May how much he needed Buck, and that Buck had saved the restaurant, despite the chef's arrogance and gruff attitude. Petey didn't say he had been trying to replace Buck at all. In fact, he'd given us the impression that Buck was irreplaceable.

But what if Buck had quit, I wondered. *Or what if Petey had known Buck was going to die that weekend? If that were true he would have needed a new head chef. Fast.*

Hannah's footsteps pounded toward the back office. She was close. I deleted the text and minimized the window. Then I darted out of the office, hid in the locker room, and exited the restaurant just after Hannah passed me by.

I held my breath until I made it out of the restaurant safely. I couldn't believe what I had just found. And I couldn't wait to see the looks on Teeny and Miss May's faces when I told them the news.

Petey had lied. And we needed to know why.

25

SENIOR LAWSUITS

I exploded around to the front of *Peter's Land and Sea* to find Teeny and Miss May already back in the pickup. I burst into the truck, excited to share my news, but they were already knee-deep in a heated conversation.

"You can't sue Hannah for real," said Miss May. "You never injured yourself on the property. Besides, she doesn't own the restaurant. Petey does, remember? Do you really want to sue Petey for an injury that doesn't exist?"

"About Petey—" I began.

"No," said Teeny. "Of course I don't want to sue Petey for no reason. I want to sue Hannah for no reason. Well, the reason is because she's rude and she deserves it. That's it. I'll sue her for being insensitive. And for elderly abuse."

"Now you want to be called old?" Miss May raised an eyebrow.

"When it suits me, I embrace my age. For discounts and lawsuits. In this case, I'd like to make my years work for me. Also at restaurants and in stores and sometimes movie theaters."

"You're not going to sue Hannah or anyone else," said Miss May. "Chelsea's back. Can we focus on that?"

"Fine. But never say never. Who knows what bone I might break on Hannah's property at some point in my life. I'm just waiting for my opportunity. Then... I'll strike."

"Can I talk now?" I said.

Miss May turned her palm up as if to give me the floor. "Please. Tell us what happened in there."

I took a deep breath and launched into the tale of my adventure inside *Land and Sea*. I didn't spare any details as I recounted what had happened. Miss May and Teeny got hung up on the lockers briefly. Teeny thought I should have tried to pick a lock and break into a locker, while Miss May disagreed and argued that picking a lock would've taken too much time.

After much debate, I got around to the computer and Petey's ad for a new chef at the restaurant. I told Miss May and Teeny that the ad had been written two days before Buck's death and they drew the same conclusion I had.

"If Petey wrote that ad before Buck died, that suggests that Petey might have been planning to kill Buck." Miss May ran her tongue over her lips. "And let's not forget Petey started as a cook himself, at *Grandma's*. So he knows how to make cinnamon buns, I'm sure."

Teeny gasped. "I taught him!"

"This theory makes sense except for one problem," I said. "My gut tells me Petey is innocent."

"Your gut is telling me the same thing," said Teeny. "Yeah, the kid is an emotional tornado. I get why he's a suspect. But he doesn't have the killer instinct. He's a lamb, not a lion."

"I know Petey worked for you and you have a soft spot for him," said Miss May. "And Chelsea, I know you like to assume the best in people. But we need to look at the facts. Not only did Petey write the ad before Buck died, he lied to us when we asked about his relationship with Buck."

"I know," I said. "But I still think it was one of the girls. Or perhaps someone we haven't thought about yet. Hannah is terrible. She was terrible that morning at the restaurant when she wouldn't let us inside. And she was really callous just now. She didn't have any sympathy for Teeny's broken ankle."

"Teeny doesn't have a broken ankle," said Miss May.

"Hannah didn't know that!" Teeny said.

"Maybe she could tell. Maybe that's why she lacked sympathy."

"Whatever," said Teeny. "The woman is sketchy. And let's not forget she lied, too. Hannah could have told us that she and Buck were separated but she kept that information to herself. Why? Probably because it would make it seem like she killed him."

"Teeny has a point," I said. "And it's still possible something went wrong between Buck and Rebecca in the last week. Why did she stop visiting Buck's hotel room after she died her hair red?"

"Maybe the hair belonged to someone else," Teeny said.

"All the evidence suggest the hair in the brush belonged to Rebecca," said Miss May. "We should go with that theory for now."

"Maybe Buck wasn't attracted to redheads," said Teeny, "so once Rebecca died her hair, he cut her off. Or maybe she got sick of visiting that disgusting hotel room. Or maybe things just ran their course."

"'Ran their course,'" I said. "That's an interesting euphemism for murder."

"So where are we?" asked Miss May. "Who is our most likely suspect?"

"I don't know what to think," I said. "Buck's life was messier than his hotel room. But Petey lied to us about Buck. And Petey seemed to know he was going to need a new chef very soon. So I think we should talk to Petey."

"I agree," said Miss May. "Teeny?"

"Fine," said Teeny with a defeated sigh. "I guess that means we're going back to the retirement community."

"Not so fast." Miss May turned to me with a small smile. "We're late for an important appointment."

I furrowed my brow. I wasn't aware that Miss May and I had an appointment, let alone an important one. And I couldn't help but wonder where we might be headed next.

26

GROOMED TO KILL

*M*iss May directed me to leave the *Land and Sea* parking lot and drive back to the farm for our 'appointment.' I was curious and a bit suspicious but I did as I was told.

And boy am I glad I followed directions!

When we pulled up to the farmhouse, a big white van was idling, waiting for us. The words "Wizard of Paws" were painted on the side of the van along with the faces of several adorable puppies and kittens. A short woman with cropped black hair was leaning against the truck.

Yes. She was even short compared to me.

"You called a mobile dog groomer," I said. "Awesome! I totally forgot KP had asked me to do that. But Steve has been so gross. Thank you!"

"Scruffy is not a good look for Steve," Miss May said.

"Totally agree," I said. "He's not a hippie dog. He's a business dog. And he likes to look sharp."

"That truck is adorable," said Teeny. "I want to get groomed in there."

Miss May laughed. "I don't think they groom human

women. But they do groom cats. So I made an appointment for Kitty, too."

"Oh my goodness," I said. "I know I should be feeling serious and morose because we're in the middle of a murder investigation. But this is going to be so cute. The cat's getting a haircut!"

I hopped out of the car and the short woman who ran the grooming truck gave me a big wave with both hands at the same time. "Hey. I'm Amy. Great to meet you."

Amy was energetic. From up close, I could see that she had bright green eyes and a tiny little nose to match her tiny little stature. Her makeup was perfect but subtle, and her A-line dress was covered in tiny little dogs.

"Great to meet you, Amy. I'm Chelsea."

Miss May and Teeny headed inside to grab Steve and Kitty while Amy and I chatted.

"OK, Chelsea," said Amy. "I have an important question for you."

"Let's hear it," I said with a laugh.

"What kind of dog are you? I have a firm belief that at their core, everybody is some kind of dog. Even cat people. So what's your breed?"

I smiled. "I'm going to have to think about that. But I know my aunt is an old German Shepherd. She's protective but fun. A little slower than she used to be, but don't tell her I said that. And our friend Teeny? The little blonde lady? She's a tough one. She's a small dog on the outside but she thinks she's much bigger. Maybe like, a Jack Russell terrier? Or a chihuahua. Don't tell her I said that, though. I don't think she'd like being called a chihuahua."

"You seem like you could be a lab. Or a doodle of some sort. You've definitely got some poodle in there."

I wasn't sure if I should take that as a compliment or an

insult. I decided to remain neutral. "What kind of dog are you, Amy?"

Amy's sparkling eyes lit up as soon as I asked the question. "Me? Well, I think some people would say I'm a bulldog. I'm stubborn and persistent. Long walks are not my thing unless there's a good reason for them. But I don't think I'm a bulldog, at least not a hundred percent. I'm a little bit more of a mix. Like maybe a bulldog and a corgi. I'm short, for one thing, like really short, I'm sure you noticed... One more inch off and I would technically be a dwarf. Also, I don't require a ton of exercise. I have a short attention span, unless I'm on the hunt for food... And I'm usually friendly. Usually being the key word."

"You seem nice to me," I said.

"Thank you. So do you. But also kind of like a know-it-all, hence the poodle comparison. Oh! That was kind of mean, wasn't it? Don't be offended, I love know-it-alls."

My head was spinning from the speed of Amy's chatter, and her ability to be so nice and so incisive in a half a breath. "Uh, right. Well, I am kind of a know-it-all, I guess. At least according to Chihuahua and German Shepherd in there. Are you new in town? I didn't know there were any dog groomers in Pine Grove, mobile or otherwise."

"I'm from California, but I've been on the east coast for a few years now. Got married fresh out of college and started grooming pets right around that time, too. Then things got sort of hairy in my personal life. Pun intended. I was married to this really tall guy, I call him 'Beanstalk' now because I don't like to say his name anymore. He was freakishly tall, like, people would stare at us on the street because we were such an odd couple. Anyway, one morning, Beanstalk went out for a dozen eggs, left a note on the counter with a little heart and everything, so sweet... and then that good-for-nothing son of a... sorry, uh, that man never came back. Left me holding the bag or whatever that expression is. It took me a few years to bounce back, then I decided to move out to New York and things turned around. I met my boyfriend, Zach. We've been together a few years now, and it's going great. And pretty recently I opened this mobile grooming truck. Not going to lie, it hasn't been that easy finding customers. So I'm super excited to meet you. I think you'll be impressed with my attention to detail, skill with animals, and general customer service. I heard you guys have a tiny horse too? I've never groomed a horse but if it has four legs, I'll cut its hair! That's my motto."

"Wow," I said. That was a lot of information in not a lot of time. I was impressed by Amy's ability to talk fast, if nothing else. "That's... terrible. I know how you feel. I got left at the altar by my fiancé and then he stole my interior design business out from under me."

"I hate hearing that," said Amy. "I'm happy I found Zach. But this is why I love animals more than people... Animals never break your heart."

Over the next few minutes, I filled out a pile of paperwork about Steve and Kitty for Amy's records. Then Amy asked me a surprising question.

"Hey, so you and your aunt and your friend solve murders, right?"

I blinked in surprise. "Yes. I'm surprised you knew that if you're not from here."

"I do a quick Google on all my new clients and their addresses before I head out for the day. I don't wanna end up driving this puppy van into some sort of sketchy situation. Anyway, I was so excited to read about the three of you. Before I came out here today, I decided I was going to keep our conversation strictly professional. But I just want to tell you how inspiring it is to know that you ladies are out there solving crimes. I wish I had a crime to solve. I think I'd be great at it."

"Thank you so much," I said. "I think you'd be great at it too. Especially if you really do have great attention to detail."

Amy opened the back of her truck. Every inch was meticulously organized and scrubbed clean. "Take a look for yourself."

I climbed in the truck and glanced around. All of Amy's tools were branded with her "Wizard of Paws" logo. There was a special area for both dogs and cats. And everything had a clean, welcoming energy that was perfect for a dog groomer.

"You're right. You are quite detail-oriented," I said.

"Thanks," said Amy as she helped me out of the truck. "So, I don't want to pry, but I'm going to anyway because that's what I do. Are you working on any fun cases right now?"

I didn't want to reveal any details about Buck's murder but I let her know we had a few suspects in a recent case, and that we were trying to find our way to the truth.

Amy must have detected that I felt unsure about who might have killed Buck because as soon as I stopped talking she offered a piece of advice. "It seems like you and your aunt are great at getting information around town and chatting with your suspects. I think if you ever feel stumped, maybe it would help to remember that at the end of the day, people really are like dogs. Sometimes they get scared around strangers. But once you calm them down and give them a treat they open right up."

Three loud barks rang out from inside the house and Steve trotted out to meet Amy. She squatted down and played with him like the two of them were old friends. Miss May and Teeny hung back. Kitty watched skeptically from Miss May's arms.

"You're a good boy," said Amy. "What a good boy. Are you ready to get clean? I bet you are. Look at your pretty eyes."

As I watched Amy play with Steve and load him into the grooming truck, I mulled over her words.

Amy was right, people were a lot like dogs. Most were nice. But some were groomed to kill.

27

FINE AS FROG HAIR

*a*fter Amy left, Miss May, Teeny, and I decided to go over to Petey's apartment for a quick conversation.

We needed to find out why Petey had created a flyer to hire Buck's replacement before Buck died. And we needed to ease our way into the conversation so Petey wouldn't feel threatened. Just like Amy had said. *All we had to do was calm him down and he might open up.*

So Miss May and I nominated Teeny to take the lead.

Teeny protested the whole drive over to Petey's place. "I'm not the lead investigator here. I'm Jenna. You do the talking, May. You're Mr. Flowers."

"If you're Jenna, who am I?" I asked.

"You're right," said Teeny. "Miss May, you're Mr. Flowers. Chelsea is Jenna. And I'm no one. I'm their cat Mr. Piggy. Mr. Piggy doesn't question suspects."

Miss May smiled wide. "You're not Mr. Piggy. You're a valuable member of the team. Besides, you mentored Petey. Remember when he was just a slacker kid scraping gum off the tables at your restaurant? You helped him become the restauranteur he is today. He trusts you. You've got to lead the way."

"Miss May is right. We need that trust," I said. "I think if Petey did something wrong... he might open up and confess to you. But he wouldn't confess anything to either of us. Probably wouldn't even tell us if he had a hangnail."

"But I feel bad," said Teeny. "Petey was a mediocre employee. He was never thorough with the gum scraping. But he's a good kid. Good head, good heart. Sure, he left my restaurant and opened up a competing spot. But I don't want the kid to go to jail. I'm sure whatever Petey did to Buck, Buck deserved it. Even though Buck was a... sweet, polite gentleman."

"Good catch," I said, noting Teeny's dedication to her 'compliment Buck' game.

"Thank you." Teeny sat up tall. "I loved wonderful, handsome Buck."

We rounded the corner and stopped in front of a little apartment building beside Pine Grove's town hall. The two-story building contained four apartments. It had white vinyl siding and forest green trim. And several American flags hung in a neat row from the second story banister.

"These apartments are adorable," said Miss May. "Pine Grove needs more apartments. What if I want to downsize one day?"

"You're going to downsize from a hundred acre farm to a miniscule apartment?" I asked.

Miss May sighed. "Who are we kidding? I love that farm. I want to be buried there."

"Speaking of which," said Teeny, "any word on that disembodied foot Steve dug up on the orchard?"

"Wayne says he's working on it, but I don't know what that means," I said. "Which apartment belongs to Petey?"

"Top left," said Miss May.

I climbed out of the car with a deep breath. "Let's see if he's home."

Petey opened the door wearing gym shorts and a tattered T-shirt. He had dark circles under his eyes and his hair was matted with grease.

"Hi." He didn't manage to open his eyes all the way when he spoke. "I've been expecting the three of you. What took you so long?"

Miss May looked over at Teeny. "Teeny?"

"Oh. Right. I'm supposed to do the talking. Hi, Petey. Poor kid. Look at you. What are you wearing?"

"What are you wearing?" Petey emphasized the word 'you' as though Teeny was also dressed in rags, but she looked cute that day in nice jeans and a collared shirt.

"Hey. Don't give me attitude, Petey. We're here to help. And for your information, these are my nice jeans. Not even from a thrift store."

Miss May nudged Teeny to remind her to be gentle. Teeny coughed and straightened up. "Sorry. Give me attitude if you want. I get it. We feel so bad about your predicament. I know how hard it is to have a scandal in your restaurant, trust me. I've had so many murderers and victims come through my place sometimes I lose count. But it helps to have people to talk to and a slice of fresh apple pie."

Petey looked up. "You brought pie?"

Miss May produced a large apple pie from her purse. "Of course we did."

Moments later, we were inside, watching as Petey ate a huge slice of apple pie in silence. He devoured the pie as though he hadn't eaten in days. As soon as he finished, Miss May cut a second slice and offered it. Petey accepted and took a huge bite. Miss May, Teeny, and I exchanged looks of concern. It was hard to tell what was wrong with Petey. But something was definitely wrong.

"So... Peter. Petey. Pete," said Teeny. "How are you feeling? Why are you so stressed?"

"What do you mean 'why'? The cops have been here five times since Buck died. Flanagan says I should turn myself in for the murder or she's going to come with a warrant."

For the first time I took a look around Petey's apartment. Wood floors. Scuffed white walls. A flatscreen TV and a futon. "There's not much to search," I said.

"I know," said Petey. "It's some kind of intimidation tactic. It's working. I'm intimidated. And scared."

Teeny patted Petey's shoulder. "You don't need to be scared. Unless you killed the Rat King. But I'm sure you didn't."

Petey took another huge bite of pie without responding. Then he spoke with his mouth full. "Everyone who worked in my restaurant saw me and Buck argue. They heard the way Buck talked to me. He was a Rat King, that's a good term for it. Yeah, I hated him. But everyone did."

"If you hated him, why didn't you fire him?" I leaned forward a bit in my chair. "You're the boss at that place. You call the shots."

"Buck turned things around. I couldn't afford to lose him. So I ate all the garbage he fed me, so to speak."

We sat in silence for a few seconds. We needed to broach the topic of Petey's want ad for a new chef but it was a delicate subject and he was in a delicate place. There was no clear path forward. So Miss May brought out her metaphorical bulldozer and created one.

"We know you created an ad to replace Buck, Petey. Before he died."

Petey choked on his bite of pie and had to wash it down with a big gulp of water. Miss May continued. "There's no use denying it. But it would be helpful if you explained to us how you knew you were going to need a replacement before he passed."

Teeny shifted her weight in her chair. "It makes it seem like you planned on killing him."

"No, no, no," said Petey. "No one was supposed to see that ad. I didn't even put it out. How did you—"

"Stay focused, Petey," said Miss May.

"It's OK, kid," said Teeny. "If you killed the guy I'm sure he deserved it. Buck was... Nevermind. Can you answer the question? "

Petey's fingers clenched around his fork. His eyes darted toward the exit. My body tightened and I prepared for a fight. But then Petey hunched over and his face reddened. "Buck quit in the middle of last week. Told me he was working one more weekend and then he'd never be back. Didn't even have the courtesy to give me a full two weeks."

"And that made you mad?" Miss May asked.

Petey tossed his fork back down on the table with a clatter. "I didn't kill him."

"But why didn't you tell us he had quit when we talked to you the day Buck died?" Teeny had to force the words out, like she was squeezing the last bit of toothpaste from a tube.

"Because I knew it would make me look guilty, alright?" Petey's eyes hopped from me, to Teeny, to Miss May. He brought both fists down on the table. "You think I did it. That's— that's— that's so insulting. Get out. Get out of my apartment."

We stood up and backed toward the door. Teeny tripped over a wayward video game controller and stumbled against the wall. "Petey... It's OK... We don't—"

Petey took a threatening step toward Teeny. "Now you're just being rude. Stepping on my Nintendo controller! I think you should go."

Teeny nodded. "Sorry. So sorry. Everything's fine, Petey. Fine as frog hair. We're going."

Miss May, Teeny and I tripped over one another as we stumbled toward the door. Then we hurried down the steps and back toward the truck. Petey stood up at the banister and yelled down to us. "Frogs don't have hair! And you're not welcome here anymore!"

We piled into the car and I started the engine. Petey called out once more. "Leave the pie!"

Miss May darted to the staircase and left the apple pie on the bottom step like she was leaving a sack of a money for a ransom payment.

The whole departure felt charged with such wild hostility it made me wonder... Could Petey have more of a criminal streak than Teeny thought? And what were we supposed to do next?

28

MAD HATTERS

I let out a trembling breath as I pulled away from Petey's building. "Teeny. Are you OK? That was crazy. Petey really yelled there at the end."

Teeny waved me away. "I've been around my share of mad hatters. I don't get shaken up by some light yelling from a scrawny little boy." Teeny spoke more loudly, back toward Petey's apartment. "Hear that, Petey? I'm not scared of you."

"You tell him, Teeny" said Miss May, looking half amused, half proud of her friend.

"It's true, though," said Teeny. "I'm not scared. I'm tough. Even tougher when Chelsea's there to back me up. Petey can yell all he wants, I doubt he's got a black belt from Master Skinner's dojo like Chelsea. Chelsea hasn't lost a fight yet."

"I've gotten lucky," I said. "And I usually have the element of surprise on my side. But the truth is I never even got my black belt."

Teeny stopped in her tracks. "You didn't?"

I shook my head. "Brown."

"Oh. Brown is fine too," said Teeny. "That's just black with a little bit of water in it."

Miss May laughed. "I don't think that's how you make brown."

"No," said Teeny. "It is. I've done it."

"So what are we thinking about Petey?" I asked.

"Well," said Teeny, "Petey says Buck quit. So at least now we know Petey didn't make the flier because he was planning on killing Buck."

"I suppose that's true," I said, "but the fact that Buck quit doesn't make Petey look any more innocent. What if Petey freaked out when Buck quit? Buck was leaving Petey in the lurch. That could be a motive for murder."

Miss May bit her lip. "That's a sound theory. But if Petey lost it and killed Buck because Buck quit... I would think that would be a crime of passion. Petey would have lost his marbles in the moment and killed Buck then and there. But this murder was premeditated, as we've said before. So that makes me think maybe Petey didn't do it."

"That's not how my brain thinks of it," I said. "The way I see it, Petey was flabbergasted the moment Buck quit. Think of the way Petey is. He's an insecure kid. He wouldn't have had the gumption or the impetus to kill Buck in that moment. But the more he thought about it, the angrier he got, that's what I think. Petey's resentment bubbled up like fruit filling through a pie crust. So maybe the day after Buck resigned... Petey started planning the murder. Looking for the right poison, gathering his baking supplies and steeling his resolve."

"So you think he did it." Teeny had her head against the window in the back seat. "It seems like you think Petey is a hundred million percent guilty."

"No," I said. "Just a theory."

"I think we need to know why Buck quit," said Teeny. "That seems important to me."

"Seems like he had serious creative differences with Petey," I volunteered. "And also like he was just an unreliable, self-centered guy. Based on Buck's attitude toward women, I'd say he had commitment issues too. Maybe he hates staying at the same restaurant too long."

Miss May shook her head. "I don't think creative differences are what drove Buck away from the restaurant. Buck was the type of guy who probably had creative differences with everyone he ever met. I think he quit working at the restaurant because he finally couldn't stand working alongside his wife and his lover every single day. Think about how tense that must have been."

"Great point," said Teeny. "*Jenna and Mr. Flowers* should have something like that. It's a pretty rich setup."

"You mean we've finally come across a scenario that hasn't been covered on one of your shows?" I asked.

"Well I haven't watched every episode," said Teeny. "There are twenty-nine seasons and only so many hours in the day."

I chuckled. "I would quit working at the restaurant if I were Buck. I mean, you're right, Miss May. Who wants to spend every day sandwiched between their wife and their secret lover?"

"Exactly," said Miss May. "My thoughts? I bet Buck wanted to get back with Hannah. Wouldn't you want to move back in with your wife if you were living out of a hotel in absolute filth like Buck was? I think Buck quit the restaurant to show Hannah that he didn't want to be with Rebecca anymore."

"If you're right, that wouldn't have made Rebecca happy," I said.

"It would have made her furious," said Miss May.

"Maybe that's why Rebecca stopped visiting Buck's hotel room about a week ago. And maybe that's why she decided to dye her hair bright red. People tend to make drastic changes in the midst of heartbreak. It makes them feel like a new person. Stronger, somehow."

"I can attest to that," said Teeny. "I wore a pink wig the entire year after my first divorce. I also started training for marathons and tried to learn French. In my mind, I was becoming a sexy, superfast, French spy with attitude. In reality... Not so much. I ran two miles and learned to say 'Bonjour,' and 'Au revoir.'"

"It's 'au revoir,'" I muttered.

"Oh shut up, Chelsea," Teeny said.

Miss May smiled. "I remember that pink wig. You didn't go anywhere without that thing."

"Oh, I know," said Teeny. "I still have it, too. Sometimes I put it on if I'm feeling spunky."

"Hold on a second," I said. "We haven't confirmed Hannah knew about Buck's affair with Rebecca. This theory only makes sense if Hannah knew that Buck and Rebecca were together."

"Add that to the list of questions," said Miss May.

I rumbled up the driveway to the farmhouse. A dark figure was crouched on the porch, hunched over some sort of object. When the person saw my headlights, they abandoned their parcel, vaulted over the porch railing, hopped on a bike, and sped into the darkness.

I jumped out of the car and ran after the mysterious person. "Get back here! Hey. Stop where you are! Who goes there?!" The person disappeared so fast I couldn't even see their outline in the darkness.

I slowed to a trot and then stopped running completely. I

turned back toward Teeny and Miss May. "Did you see that? Someone was here. Maybe we should call the police."

Miss May held up her hand to calm me. "Relax. Before we do anything else let's go see what that person left on our porch..."

29

WRAPPING UP A CLUE

A pink pastry box sat in the illuminated circle created by our porch light. The box had been tied with a pretty string and there was a note attached to the top.

Miss May read the note aloud, "Hello Comrade, I have information that will bring to light to part of the investigation of for murder which you conduct."

"This person doesn't speak good English," said Teeny.

"Keep reading," I said.

"Meet at 10 Gravers Court. Kingston, New York. Tomorrow, 8 AM. Long live Russia. Signed, Wouldn't You Like to Know."

Miss May folded the note and put it in her pocket. "Someone has a tip for us. Have either of you ever met a Russian person?"

Teeny shook her head. "Not in real life."

"What other life would Miss May be talking about?" I asked. "You think she was wondering if either of us had ever met a Russian person in our dreams? In virtual reality? In a hypnotic trance?"

"Do you really want to get into that right now?" asked Teeny.

"Let's see what's in the box." Miss May scooped up the pink pastry box and untied the string with a single pull. She opened the box to reveal four perfect little pastries that looked like donuts.

"Yum." I reached out to take one. Miss May smacked my hand away.

"I don't think we should eat these," she said. "They're dusted with cinnamon and coated in sweet cream. I think these are some kind of Russian cinnamon bun."

Teeny dropped her jaw. "You think they're poisoned?!"

Miss May lowered her nose to the box and sniffed. "I have no idea."

The next morning, we piled into my pickup truck and I drove up to Kingston, New York. If you've never been to Kingston, I would recommend it. Kingston is an old Revolutionary War town, filled with ancient brick houses, historical plaques and big, beautiful trees.

The little city had a strong enclave of artists and writers who kept the streets interesting, lively, and packed with funky bars and restaurants. But there was also a quiet, studious energy that permeated the town, sort of a holdover from the kind of pensive and serious talks I imagined took place among the founding fathers during the American Revolution.

The address on the note, 10 Gravers Court, led us to a little neighborhood restaurant on the ground floor of an apartment building. The restaurant was called *Old Dancing Bear.* A huge wooden bear stood out front, grinning with its big wooden teeth and wearing a fur hat. A neon sign let us know the place was already open.

"Looks like a Russian restaurant if I've ever seen one," Teeny said.

"Let's remember to be cautious and stay aware of our surroundings in there," said Miss May. "This could be anything. It could be an ambush."

We entered to find a wood-paneled room with a dingy bar and several sturdy, wooden tables. Russian flags and other Russian memorabilia hung on the walls and music that sounded like a depressing funeral march played over hidden speakers.

A bearded man stood behind the bar wearing an apron. I approached him, assuming he was the 'comrade' we were there to meet. But the man gestured toward the front corner of the room with his head as I approached. I turned and there sat a 400-pound Russian man who was bald everywhere except for the temples. He wore a navy blue sweatsuit. And he had a large, gold watch on his plump wrist.

I nudged Miss May. "That must be who we're here to meet."

Miss May grabbed my hand. "You lead the way."

The man stood, with great effort, as we approached. He spoke with a thick Russian accent. His voice was heavy and deep, like his words were moving in slow motion. "Ladies. You received my note. Good. You are good people and good detectives. Thank you for coming."

I scrunched up my nose. "That was you on the bicycle last night?" The person on the bike had seemed significantly smaller and more limber than the specimen that stood in front of us at the *Old Dancing Bear.*

The man shook his head. "Please, no. That was an associate. He makes all my deliveries. I am pleased to see he did a good job. Please, sit."

The large man waited for us to take our seats and then he sat back down himself, again with a monumental effort.

Teeny put her palms down on the table and looked the man in the eye. "Alright, pal. Let's get down to it. Do you know who killed this guy Buck? Because we got a lot investigating to do and this bear restaurant is kind of out of the way. So we need to hit the road."

Now Teeny seemed perfectly happy to be the one doing the talking. Miss May cleared her throat and offered up her best smile to the large man. "What my friend means is thank you for inviting us here today. What can we do for you?"

When the man responded, he spoke in a higher-pitched, softer voice — the voice of a young woman. "You guys. It's me."

I laughed. Of course. The old Russian man was Liz, the editor of the *Pine Grove Gazette*, in her most elaborate disguise yet. This wasn't the first time Liz had gone undercover and pretended to be a Russian, and somehow I doubted it would be the last.

Miss May leaned forward and squinted. "Liz? You're buried in all that man?"

"Shhh! Quiet. You'll blow my identity. I can't let Yuri know this is a disguise. He thinks I'm a long-lost cousin so he lets me use this place without buying anything. There are some Russian mafia connections in Kingston. So I hang out here to try to pick up information. I'm thinking about putting together an exposé on organized crime in upstate New York and this is my foothold. I figured it would also be a good spot for us to meet. To avoid the prying eyes of Pine Grove."

"You're still going for that Pulitzer," said Teeny. "I like that. You'll get one soon. I think probably next month."

"They only give out one a year," said Liz.

"Well you know what I mean," said Teeny.

I leaned back in my chair and felt my vertebrae relax a little. I hadn't realized how tense the *Old Dancing Bear* and the large Russian man had made me. "So what's up, Liz? What do you need to talk about?"

Liz leaned forward and whispered. "You like this disguise, right? I think it's my best one yet. The fat suit cost me two grand but I think it was worth it."

"Two thousand dollars?!" I looked down as Liz glared at me. "I mean, wow. That cheap, huh?"

"It's a fine disguise," said Teeny, "but I can't believe you put on all that weight and don't even get to enjoy any of the calories."

"If I actually ate the food and got fat it wouldn't be a disguise anymore. I would just be fat."

"Fine. It's a good disguise," said Teeny. "Well worth all that money. Not a waste at all."

"Liz," said Miss May in her most patient voice. "We all love the disguise. You did a great job and you fooled us. But I'm itching to find out if you have information that can help us catch this killer. Every second we're here talking about your transformation into a grossly overweight Russian man is a second the murderer could be getting closer to claiming a second victim."

Liz nodded. "Right. Well, I'm not here with information about the murderer. But I do think I have something that might help... You know how *Peter's Land and Sea* has been really popular the last couple months?"

We nodded. Teeny cringed. She knew better than anyone.

"Yeah. Well apparently the food there has been making people sick. It's been happening pretty consistently over the past few weeks."

"Sick how?" I asked.

"Like really sick. Vomiting and everything."

I adjusted my position in my seat. "That's strange. I haven't heard anything about people getting sick. And the restaurant has only gotten more popular from one weekend to the next."

"That's what I'm saying," said Liz. "I found a few sources who confirmed that there had been illnesses that can be traced back to the restaurant. A significant number of illnesses. But I had to do serious investigative journalism just to gather that kernel of information, which is strange because usually when a restaurant makes someone sick, everyone finds out fast, especially in Pine Grove. Remember when everyone got Divola-ed?"

"Of course," I said. "Poor *Divola's* is still recovering."

"It is curious that none of us have heard a peep about food poisoning or sickness from Petey's," said Miss May. "I don't suppose you can reveal who your sources are?"

Liz shook her big, old, Russian head. Her fake jowls wobbled. "Not a chance."

Miss May scratched her chin. "It seems to me if the food was making people sick but no one talked about it... That means someone was keeping people quiet somehow." She looked up at Liz. "This is a real conspiracy.

"I knew that dirty rat wasn't the world-class chef he pretended to be," said Teeny.

"Teeny," I said, "I thought you were only saying nice things about Buck."

"Sorry. Um... I knew that amazing man was going to poison people... No. It doesn't work because I can't pretend the food isn't poisoning people. Sorry. In this case, he's a Rat King."

Liz leaned forward. "Do you think this will help with your investigation?"

Miss May nodded. "It's an interesting development. And it gives me a lot of ideas about what we may need to do next."

30

THE PROOF IS IN THE POISONED PUDDING

"Unfortunately, this further strengthens Petey's motive for the murder." Miss May pushed open the door to a little organic market in Kingston and stepped inside. Teeny and I followed.

"I thought the same thing. If Buck was making people sick at Petey's restaurant and hiding it... That would have made Petey pretty angry." I said. "But you think Liz's sources are reliable? I mean, it's all hearsay."

"She hasn't led us in the wrong direction before, so for now let's assume she was reporting accurate information." Miss May pointed to the back of the store. "Look. There's a little sandwich counter back there. Maybe we can grab a bite before we head home."

I looked around the market and for the first time registered my surroundings. The place was small. Cluttered with organic, healthy snacks and healthy meat substitutes, like chick'n cutlets made from soy protein. There was a small produce area with fresh fruits and vegetables, which all seemed refreshingly irregular in shape and color. And, just as Miss May had pointed out, there was a small sandwich counter in the back with an eclectic, handwritten menu. "Sure. I could go for a snack. I also want to know more about what you think about Buck and the restaurant and the low-key food poisoning epidemic."

"OK," said Miss May. "So let's assume Buck's food really made people sick. Maybe Buck somehow convinced the first batch of people not to tell anyone. But he's been a chef a long time. He knows better than anyone that word gets out. So, maybe he decided to make a run for it because he knew the food poisoning scandal was going to ruin his reputation. I think Buck quit *Peter's Land and Sea* because he wanted to leave town and get a new job before word of his rotten cooking made it out of Pine Grove."

Teeny shook her head. "If you've got a restaurant and your food makes people sick, it's not good. If one of my cooks was irresponsible enough to use bad ingredients, I'd be mad. Real mad."

Miss May nodded. "I know. It's hard to recover from something like that. Like with *Divola's*. It takes years to reha-bilitate your image, even if only one or two people are affected. Imagine if Petey found out that Buck's cooking had made so many customers sick at the restaurant? I think Petey would get mad too. The kid is emotional. Impulsive. Soft-hearted maybe, but I think he has a temper. Petey risked his reputation and spent his entire savings on *Peter's Land and Sea*. Something like this could bankrupt any restaurant owner."

"True, but let's not get ahead of ourselves," I said. "I want to think about all the angles."

"What other angles do you see?" said Miss May.

"Buck has been a chef a long time," I said. "What if his food has made people sick before? What if Buck's cooking bankrupted the owner of a restaurant where he'd previously

worked? Maybe Buck ruined someone's business in some
other town, and then he ran to Pine Grove to get a new job
and hide in the country. But then *Peter's Land and Sea* got
popular and the owner of the previous restaurant found out,
hunted Buck down, and killed him."

Teeny turned down the sides of her mouth. "Makes
sense to me. Guys like that, with all those tattoos, always
have a checkered past. For goodness sake, I don't even know
Buck's last name."

"I thought Buck was his last name," I said. "But I guess
maybe Buck is a nickname. Maybe we don't know any of his
real names."

"I hadn't thought about it at all," said Miss May. "But you
do bring up a good point, Chelsea. If Buck bankrupted or
otherwise damaged a previous restaurant, that owner might
have carried out a vendetta. Or what if Buck's cooking killed
someone in his previous job? Maybe there's an angry spouse
left behind who wants revenge? This opens up a whole new
world of possible suspects."

"So we need to find out more about Buck's cooking
skills," I said. "If he has made people sick at his previous
jobs, then there might be a long list of revenge-seeking
killers who wanted him dead. Or someone he sickened in
Pine Grove might want him dead for the same reason."

"Do either of you know where Buck worked before
this?" asked Miss May, headed toward the sandwich counter
in the back of the store.

"No idea," Teeny said. "But I hope you're in the mood for
a vegetarian sandwich with lots of micro sprouts or whatever because that's all this place has."

"I'm in the mood for vegetarian all the time," said Miss
May. "I'm healthy, remember? I walked to *Grandma's*."

"I was there when you arrived," said Teeny. "You were very tired."

"It was a long walk."

We took a break from our conversation to quickly order sandwiches, then we stepped aside and continued where we'd left off. "If we want to find out where Buck worked before *Peter's*," I said, "I bet you Petey knows."

Teeny pointed at me with a little grin. "You're right. I'll get Petey on the phone."

Miss May pulled a smart phone from her purse. "You sure you don't want me to call? Petey seemed pretty upset with you yesterday.

"I told you, I don't care about that. My feathers weren't even a little bit ruffled." Teeny dialed and waited. "Petey? Hi. It's fine. Really, it's fine." She waited a few seconds and nodded as she listened. "You don't have to apologize."

Teeny laughed as Petey spoke. "Exactly. You're too skinny and weak to take Chelsea in a fight. And you don't know anything about karate. Anyway, enough small talk. We need to know where Buck worked before you hired him. What you mean you don't know? Oh right. His resume was the fact that he cooked you a good omelette. Well do you have any information that might help us figure out where he worked before he came to Pine Grove? His last name is Johnson? Figures. Ugh. There must be a million Johnsons out— Oh, what? Really? Great. That's exactly what I needed."

Teeny hung up. "Buck Johnson studied at the renowned *Culinary Institute of America*."

Miss May smirked. "That's on our way home."

Teeny mirrored Miss May's smirk exactly. "I know."

31

COOKING UP TROUBLE

*T*he *Culinary Institute of America* was located along the Hudson River in a town called Hyde Park, New York. Like many of the towns along the Hudson, Hyde Park was rich with history and a plethora of beautiful homes to match. Perhaps Hyde Park's most notable claim to fame was that the town had once been home to Franklin D. Roosevelt. As a result, there were several sites dedicated to Roosevelt, including a preserved historic home, a presidential library and a museum.

As I drove into the town, I kept getting distracted by the gorgeous foliage and stately old homes.

What is it about old houses that delight people so much?

For me, old buildings provided a sense of security, and a hopefulness about humanity. It's comforting to see giant structures that had survived decades if not centuries of change. The structures, settled and sturdy, reminded me to remain calm and collected in stressful situations, because time presses on and there's no point worrying about things you can't control.

Miss May pointed me up a giant hill, which led directly

to the *Culinary Institute of America*, a gorgeous campus often referred to as the 'Majesty on the Hudson.'

My jaw dropped as we came upon manicured lawns and lush hillside. There had to be a hundred acres at least. Then we came to the main building, a five story brick structure with Greek or Roman columns flanking a gorgeous front door. As an interior designer, I should've known the difference between Doric, Ionic, and Corinthian columns but at that particular moment, I didn't feel like using my brain to distinguish the details of the architecture. There was too much to look at.

"This place is breathtaking," I said. "I can't breathe. It's stealing my breath."

"I've never taken you here?" asked Miss May.

I shook my head.

"I should have. Teeny and I have taken a few cooking classes up here over the years. And we've come to the restaurant a few times."

"The restaurants are so fun, Chelsea," said Teeny. "They're all run by the students here. So the cooks are studying cooking, of course. But the rest of the staff is comprised of *Culinary Institute* students, too. The hostess, the waiters, the dishwashers... The whole dining experience has this energy of youthful exuberance and experimentation and it's so wonderful and vibrant. We have to come back sometime. I think there's an Italian restaurant near the bottom of the hill. That's my favorite."

"Mine too," said Miss May. "And the prices are slightly more affordable than they would be elsewhere, probably because everything is prepared by students. But you would never know the difference. These kids are so talented... Their cooking is better than anything you can get in most of the country."

Teeny cleared her throat.

"Except for at *Grandma's,* of course," Miss May said.

"You two sound like a brochure for the *Culinary Institute of America*," I said with a chuckle. "I love it! And I guess all that means Buck has real skill in the kitchen."

"Oh yeah," said Teeny.

"That's so strange though," I said. "Sounds to me like everyone who attends this school is a good chef. So how does someone from this revered institution turn out food that makes customers sick in his restaurant?"

"Even the best schools have one or two dunces," said Teeny. "You know, those kids who have to wear the big hats and sit in the corner while the teacher calls them dumb?"

"I don't think they do that in schools anymore," I said.

"Well that's good," said Teeny. "Those hats are itchy. And sometimes the teacher makes you wear it just for talking during class. You don't have to be stupid to talk during class! Not that I would know."

Miss May laughed. "Either way, Buck didn't strike me as a dunce. I bet he just got lazy over the years. Or sloppy."

"Sloppy sounds right," said Teeny. "If you don't practice what you learn, you lose it. I realized that when I was studying French. So many of my language skills went into my brain, out my ear, and around the corner never to be seen or heard from again."

I laughed and parked the car, ready for intense investigation. And maybe some good food.

The three of us signed in as visitors at the big main building, then we hopped onto a tour that appeared to be populated by prospective students.

The tour guide was a chubby, plucky young man wearing a chef's coat over his jeans. The kid had a big smile and he beamed with pride when he spoke of the *Institute* and its rigorous curriculum in baking, sauce making, and all other forms of cooking.

"I should have applied to come here," said Teeny. "This seems like a real party."

"You still can," I said.

"Yeah, right." Teeny raised her hand and the chubby tour guide called on her. "Excuse me! Hi! Yup. Back here. The short one. Great to meet you. My name is Teeny and I was just wondering... How old is the oldest student currently enrolled at the *Institute*?"

"Great question, Tiny," said the tour guide. "The vast majority of students here are college-aged but we do have one older student among us, a thirty-something lawyer who is hoping to change careers and open a restaurant after graduation. She is a magician with poultry and fowl."

"That's what I thought, thanks," said Teeny. "Also, it's Teeny. Not Tiny."

The tour guide offered a quick mea culpa, then led our group further down the hall. Miss May leaned in toward me. "We need to find someone who might have known Buck when he was a student. A professor, probably. I'm thinking one of us should sneak into a class."

"You heard the tour guide," said Teeny. "You and I are too old to be students here. If someone's sneaking into a class at the *Culinary Institute* and posing as a student, it's going to have to be Chelsea."

Miss May and Teeny loved shoving me into precarious situations and watching me flail. Typically, I hated their suggestions. Like, one time, they made me pretend to be a masseuse and massage some guy's hairy back just to ask him a few questions. But in this case, I didn't mind the ruse at all. I had loved my time at college, and I considered myself a master of pretending to know what was going on in a class even when I was deeply, deeply confused.

I smiled. "OK. I'll check out a class. We should try to find something about gourmet French cooking, I think. Buck was snooty about his food, so I think the professor of a snooty class is most likely to remember him."

Miss May nodded. "Good thinking. Keep your eyes peeled."

As the tour continued, I noticed that every student wore a chef's coat identical to the one donned by our tour guide. I spotted one of the coats hanging over a chair in an empty classroom, darted inside, and put it on. When I returned to the tour group Miss May and Teeny smiled. "You look you're ready for class."

"That's the goal," I said. "I'm going to split off from the group and see if I can find that French cooking class. Have fun on the rest of the tour."

As I finished my sentence a group of students drifted by like a school of fish. I slid into the middle of the group, anonymous in my white coat, and hurried along with them.

Although it took significant searching, and I had to join two new schools of fish on my journey, I soon found a class on classical French cooking that was scheduled to begin in five minutes. I slipped inside and took a seat in the back. Perfect.

Or, as they French would say, *parfait!*

32

FRENCH LESSONS

*T*he classroom was equipped with a few rows of large desks that each had a small stove and sink built into the countertop. I selected a desk near the back and wiggled with excitement as I played with the faucet and twisted the knobs on the stove.

Over the course of the next few minutes, the room filled with students, chatting, laughing, and prepping for class.

Then an acne-scarred young man took the seat next to me. He cocked his head and looked at me with curiosity. "Hi. Sorry. Who are you?"

"Hi. Great to meet you. I'm new here. I transferred from the... *Culinary Institute of Canada.*"

"Is your name is Michael?" Tim pointed at the name embroidered on the chest of my chef's coat. I hadn't even noticed it until he pointed out. Sure enough, the name was Michael.

I thought on my feet, which was impressive, since I had shoved them both in my mouth with my bizarre lie about the CIA's Canadian corollary.

"Technically it's pronounced the French-Canadian way,

'Michel.' But you can call me Michael. Or Mike for short. It's a pretty common name for girls in Canada. You'd be surprised."

"My name's Tim," said my classmate. "It's weird that you're starting here in the middle of the semester."

I let out a nervous laugh. "I had to pull a lot of strings to make that happen. But I'm so happy to be here and thrilled to meet you, Tim. How do you like this class? How's the professor?"

Tim winced. "This is the hardest class at the *Institute*. They say it separates the chefs from the cooks. A lot of kids drop out after they take this class and go home to work on their family farm or whatever. I get so scared before this class every week that I have to throw up in the hallway bathroom before it starts. No one warned you about Chef P?"

I shook my head. Felt my palms begin to sweat. Oh no.

"Apparently his name is so long and French that no one has ever been able to pronounce it, not even his parents, so people just call him 'Chef P.' He's mean, Michael. Real mean. Try to stay under the radar if you can."

A tall, skinny man with a pointy chin entered and stood in the front of the class. Tim gulped and sat up straight. The entire class greeted Chef P. Chef P honed right in on me.

"Who are you, girl?" He spoke in a thick French accent and his chin got even pointier with each word he spoke.

"Oh. I'm Michael."

"Michel?"

"Yeah. I'm French-Canadian. So you can pronounce it either way."

Chef P smacked the counter in front of him with a spatula. "Your coat says Michael! I will call you Michael if your name is Michael."

I explained my story about being a transfer student and Chef P seemed to buy it.

"Oh. Fancy Michael is from the *Culinary Institute of Canada*. I bet you think that makes you better than us, don't you? OK. You think you're so tough? Today we are learning how to cook an exquisite French ratatouille. Tell me how to begin."

"Right. Ratatouille..." The word meant little more to me than any French word. I knew it was something about vegetables. I bit my lip and wished Teeny or Miss May was there to help. "It's a French food. Lots of veggies. And there was a movie about it where a rat—"

Slap! Chef P smacked the counter once more with his dreaded spatula. "Stop talking. No one shall reference that movie in my class. It is an abomination to French cooking and I will not have it spoken of. Now can anyone help Michael, who struggles so spectacularly to define even such a basic meal?"

Tim raised his hand and spoke in a squeaky voice. "Ratatouille is a French Provençal stewed vegetable dish that originated in Nice. Recipes and cooking times differ but common ingredients include tomato, garlic, zucchini, eggplant, pepper, and a healthy combination of leafy green herbs."

Chef P gave Tim a sarcastic round of applause. Then the chef charged forward with his lesson, chopping vegetables faster than anyone I had ever seen and cooking almost on autopilot as he rambled about the varieties of ratatouille and the importance of cooking each vegetable separately and then combining at the end.

Tim chopped almost as fast as Chef P. I, on the other hand, barely got through half my vegetables by the end of the hour-long course. But I managed to avoid more of Chef

P's ire, which I believe emanated from the tip of his diabolical chin, until the class ended.

I waited for all the other students to trickle out and then approached Chef P with my head hung in deference. "Chef P?"

The chef did not look up from his cleanup efforts at his station. "What is it, Michael? Don't offend me with any stupidity. I will not tolerate ignorance in my presence. Nor will any French person."

"I just want to say it was great to meet you. I'm honored to be a student in your class. My friend, Buck Johnson, told me you're the best teacher in the world for French cooking. He, uh, he actually wrote the recommendation letter that got me into this school. I just want to say I'm happy to be here. Thank you for everything you do," I said, adding an "eh?" to emphasize my Canadian roots.

Chef P put down his knife with a slow and careful motion. He made eye contact with me. "You know Buck Johnson."

It was hard for me to tell from the look in the chef's eyes whether or not knowing Buck was a good thing or a bad thing. I gave him a tiny nod of the head.

"He was a brilliant student here. Buck Johnson is a horribly ugly name. Grotesque. Saying it made my tongue writhe with the agony of the mundane. Buck Johnson. Uch. No elegance to it at all. But he was one of my star pupils."

"Yeah. I figured you would say that. Buck is a great cook... and I also admire that he always insists on safe food preparation. He has a lot of integrity when it comes to stuff like that. He's never made a single person sick with his food. Not that I know of."

Chef P bristled. "Of course Buck Johnson hasn't made anyone sick with his food. No graduate of the *Culinary Insti-*

tute of America sickens his or her diners. But why do you say such a thing?"

"Sorry. I don't know."

"Think before you speak, Michael."

"I will. So... Buck was a star student, huh? He always told me he did well here but I never knew how much of that was true."

"He did very well."

"I guess that's why he's had so much success as a chef over the years," I said. "I would love to have a career like his. But Buck has never told me about the path he took after graduation."

"He was being modest," said Chef P. "Humility is the worst of all American traits. What is the point of accomplishing great things if you neglect to talk about them? Buck Johnson was hired immediately after graduation at *Hudgens* restaurant in New York City. Manhattan." Chef P stared into the distance with a faraway look in his eyes. "He was the envy of every student at the *Institute*. He started as a cook in the kitchen, I believe. But within one or two years he had risen to the position of head chef at *Hudgens*. That's a magnificent achievement for anyone, let alone a recent graduate. *Hudgens* is unparalleled in the culinary world."

"*Hudgens*," I repeated.

"Stop repeating me, Michael. Now depart from my presence. Another class is about to start."

I gave Chef P a respectful bow of the head and hurried out of the classroom. I wondered how Buck Johnson had fallen from glory at *Hudgens Restaurant* and ended up in Pine Grove.

And how had such a renowned and promising chef produced food that had made so many people sick?

33

SNAKE OIL SALESWOMAN

*M*iss May, Teeny and I agreed we needed more information about Buck and his career as a chef. So we decided that on the following day, we would trek down to New York City to check out *Hudgens* and see what we could learn.

We had so many questions they were hard to track.

Had Buck made people sick with his cooking while working at *Hudgens*? Better yet, had he angered anyone? Had he created any enemies? And was there someone at his previous job who may have wanted to kill him?

The idea of doing investigative work in New York City shot an electric tingle through my fingers and toes like a burst of static. Our visits to New York for past investigations had always been strange and wonderful and I was confident our upcoming visit would be more of the same.

Something about the city smells like intrigue. Maybe it's the steam that rises from the sewer grates or the anonymity of the crowds or the mere fun of being someplace new. I couldn't say for sure. But I barely got any sleep that night as images of the Big Apple looped through my mind.

I got out of bed the next morning to find the farmhouse quiet and empty. Steve the dog was lying beside the fireplace where a few remaining embers crackled and died. I crouched beside him. "Hey Steve. Looking pretty sharp with your new haircut. Like you're ready for your first day on Wall Street."

Steve wasn't in the mood to talk. In fact, he didn't bother to wake up at the sound of my voice. So I patted his haunch and headed onto the front porch. I could see Miss May and KP out in the orchard, pointing at the trees and gesticulating to indicate excitement. I pulled on a pair of shoes, teetering as I tried to stand on one leg, then the other. Then I trudged out to see what the two of them were talking about.

"What's with the meeting of the minds?" I asked.

"Nothing, according to me," KP grunted.

"What about according to you?" I said to Miss May.

Miss May shook her head. "The second weekend of October is the best weekend of the year for picking Red Delicious and Golden Delicious apples. This whole section of trees here consists of Red Delicious and Golden Delicious. So we planned well. Although I didn't plant the trees, my great-grandfather did, so I can't take much credit."

"Yeah now tell her the problem," said KP.

Miss May plucked a Red Delicious from a tree and held it out for me to see. "I don't think this apple looks plump enough."

"It's plump," said KP. "You just don't remember. This is what they're like every single year. We can't change it now, anyway, so who cares? The apples aren't gonna get any fatter just 'cuz you're mad at 'em."

"I don't want to get a reputation for having apples that are small and lacking juiciness," said Miss May. "If they're not plump, we should take note of it and figure out how we can change things next year."

"How about we let the people decide?" said KP. "That's what I say. If the apples are too measly and skinny, we'll hear about it. The customers at this place complain more than a reindeer in the desert."

"Why would a reindeer..." KP shot me a look and I changed course. "I agree with KP. Also, Miss May, we're supposed to go down to the city this morning, remember? Not that I don't respect your diligence on the farm, that's very admirable... But we're supposed to go to *Hudgens*."

"I heard that place is good," said KP. "Too swanky for me. Me and fancy don't mix."

"How have you heard about a five-star New York City restaurant?" I asked.

"*Food Network*, thank you very much," KP retorted. "Me and TV get along just fine."

"We'll go soon," Miss May said to me. "I only have a few more issues I need to discuss with KP."

Miss May dragged KP further out into the orchard, listing off her concerns as they walked. He threw a glance back at me over his shoulder, like, "Please help," and I laughed.

As the two of them disappeared into the trees, I watched my hot breath form in the cold air. At that moment, Miss May's attention to detail on the orchard was delaying our much-anticipated trip to the city. It would have been easy for me to begrudge her that, except that the same attention to detail had proven useful in so many cases... *Just as it would in the case of the murdered chef.*

We finally got on the road at around noon, picked Teeny up from *Grandma's,* and headed down to the city. It was a beautiful ride, as it often is. Miles and miles of trees, dressed in their fall plumage, eventually gave way to the big, brown buildings of the Bronx and then the enormous skyscrapers of Manhattan. Miss May had insisted on driving her Volkswagen bus, so I feared we wouldn't be able to find parking. But we got lucky on that front and found a spot just a few blocks away from *Hudgens*.

It turned out the great parking spot didn't matter much, because *Hudgens* was closed for lunch and wouldn't reopen again until 5 PM for dinner service.

Much to the amazement of Teeny and Miss May, I made a reservation for 5 PM using the Internet. But that meant we still had about three hours to kill so we headed off for a ladies' afternoon in Manhattan.

We were in a neighborhood called the West Village, which is one of New York's trendiest, and most expensive, hot spots. The streets were lined with beautiful old brownstones and big oak and maple trees. And there was a café, bistro, or bar on every corner.

Teeny looked down a long line of apartment buildings and scratched her head. "I swear I lived on this street for a few months in my twenties. But which building was it?"

"No one is going to figure that out but you," said Miss May. "I forgot you lived here at all! That wasn't your pink hair phase, was it?"

"Oh no, that was much later. I lived in the city during my hippie phase. Although I wasn't very good at being a hippie. I spent most of my time walking around and looking at all the hippies."

"Good training for life as an amateur sleuth," I said.

Teeny turned the corner and stood bolt upright. "There it is. That's the building." She hurried down the block. Then she turned and walked back toward me and Miss May. "Nevermind. False alarm. These buildings all look alike."

The three of us decided to kill time with a cup of coffee at a hip coffee shop called *The Dinosaur Cafe*. The place featured sharp minimalist design, with high ceilings, white walls, and a few big pops of color, like a neon sign framed by a living wall of ferns. My interior design brain briefly went into hyperdrive as I imagined a few ways to improve the place — a well-placed shelf of merchandise, or a silhouette of the company logo on the door — but I refrained from mentioning to the cranky barista the ways in which I thought their decorating could improve. Probably for the best, I thought, since the process of ordering my cup of coffee seemed to get on the barista's last nerve.

There's that famous hipster service you hear all about.

After the three of us ordered our coffees, we took a seat outside. As Teeny and Miss May chatted about folks they knew who had moved into or out of the city, I noticed an interesting shop across the street and a little ways down.

"Look at that place," I said. "It's an apothecary. I told you they're popping up all over the city. I bet Rebecca tries to sell her oils and tinctures and creams to places like that."

"Seems like we should check it out," said Miss May.

I smiled. "Couldn't agree more."

The apothecary had a minimalist appearance very similar to the style featured at *Dinosaur*. It had bright white walls and there were just a few jars dotting every shelf. Each jar had a little plaque in front of it that stated the price: $45 for "eye balm," $75 for "rejuvenation formula," $55 for a jar of something called "Better Sleep."

Miss May nudged me. "Check that out. More sleep for only $55? Not so bad."

"'Better sleep,'" I said. "Whatever that means."

A trim young woman in high-waisted jeans and a crop top sashayed toward us. "Oh my God, you two are looking at the 'Better Sleep?' That is our best product. I put four drops on my tongue every night before bed and I've definitely been sleeping better. I could get you our smaller bottle for $40 if you'd like to try it out."

"We're OK for now." Miss May picked up the bottle and turned it over to read the label. "But I see here there are only a couple of ingredients listed, and then the label just says, 'and other ingredients.' Why is that?"

"Oh, right," said the woman. "Yeah, so apothecaries are not, like, regulated by any government agencies or whatever, so ingredients can be hard to come by."

"You have no idea what's in it?" Miss May asked.

"The owner here has personally tried everything on the shelf and she loves it all," said the girl. "And I can vouch for it too."

"But..."

"Yeah. I'm not positive what all the ingredients are."

"What if people have allergies?" Miss May asked.

"Or what if it's toxic?" I added.

"Yeah, so I understand your concerns but we use all natural ingredients. I mean, sure, trace amounts of poison are in everything, right? Even like, the water. But--"

"That sounds wrong to me," I said.

The salesgirl bristled and her tone sharpened. "We recommend anyone with severe allergies avoid using our products. Do you have severe allergies?"

"What about this ingredient?" I asked, pointing to one of the labels. "Cassava?"

"That's one of our secrets. So good for your neck lines. Let me know if you'd like some." She gave me a tight smile and bopped away.

I frowned and turned to Miss May. "Is something wrong with my neck?"

"No, Chelsea. Your neck is beautiful."

Teeny approached from across the store. "Are you two thinking what I'm thinking?"

I nodded.

Teeny smiled wide. "$55 is a great price for more sleep."

"'Better sleep,'" I said with a groan.

Teeny responded with an excited speech about the value of sleep. But her voice dulled in my mind as my I mulled over what the salesgirl had said about her products and a sense of dread climbed up my belly and into my heart.

"Trace amounts of poison are in everything... right?"

34

HUDGENS HUZZAH

*H*udgens restaurant was the fanciest place I'd ever been in my entire life. It wasn't a large restaurant, just one square room, but every detail screamed understated luxury.

The hostess stand seemed to be carved from the same marble as the statue of *David*. A pianist with the hands of Liberace played jazz standards on a Steinway. The plates were trimmed in real gold. And I'm pretty sure there was an actual Picasso hanging on the wall.

When we first entered the restaurant, I felt self-conscious in my normal-people clothes. No one had told me I would need to wear an evening gown to dinner, after all. But I straightened my shoulders and tipped my nose toward the ceiling as we walked to our table, and by the time we were seated I had forgotten all about my insecurities.

I sat in my fancy chair, laid my silken napkin across my lap, and perused the gourmet menu like Queen Elizabeth herself.

I ordered butternut squash soup to start, topped with

fresh toasted pumpkin seeds and extra virgin olive oil. For dinner, I got homemade pappardelle in a sun-dried tomato sauce that had a wonderful, peppery aftertaste. I'd never experienced the literal sensation of something melting in my mouth before, but I swear, I didn't even have to chew.

Miss May and Teeny got food too, of course. But I was so involved in mine, I had no idea what they ordered or whether or not they even liked it.

When the three of us realized that we were in for a fine dining experience, we decided to hold off on questioning anyone at the restaurant until after our meal. We didn't want them to tamper with our food. More importantly, we wanted to savor every carefully curated bite.

Even amateur sleuths deserve to be treated like royalty sometimes, right?

Our waitress was a beautiful, middle-aged woman with perfect posture and a dainty gold bracelet. We didn't mention the name Buck Johnson to her until the very end of the meal. Then, finally, Miss May broached the subject as the woman cleared our plates.

"Did you know Buck Johnson when he worked here?" she asked. "I think he was head chef."

"I'm fairly new to the restaurant, ma'am," said the woman. "Prior to this, I worked aboard luxury cruise ships. Prior to that, I was a server at the White House. It's been quite the journey but *Hudgens* is where I feel most at home. Everything here is of the finest order."

Miss May thanked the woman and we waited on the check. After a few minutes, the hand with the gold bracelet gently laid the bill on our table in a fine leather case. I snatched it up and slid my credit card inside. Miss May and Teeny protested but it was too late. I had already handed the heavy leather case to the server.

"Let me pay for this," I insisted. "You two are both like mothers to me, and we've never once celebrated Mother's Day all together. Consider this a few years of restitution. You've both given me so many nice experiences in my life."

"Chelsea. You don't have to do this," said Miss May.

Teeny nudged Miss May dramatically. "May. Quiet down. We're about to get a free dinner."

I laughed. "For real. Thank you both. And to you especially, Miss May. You've given me a job and a true home. I'm grateful for that."

Miss May was not an emotional woman, but she dabbed gently at her eyes with her napkin. Before she could respond, a husky voice interrupted our tender moment.

"Good evening, ladies." A stocky, bearded man in a crisp blazer stood before us.

"My name is Jeffrey and I'm the owner of this restaurant," the man said. "Was everything to your liking this evening?"

Miss May, Teeny, and I responded with a chorus of, "Yes. Amazing. So good."

Jeffrey looked pleased but there was an uneasy look in his eyes. "Wonderful. And I heard you were asking after our former chef, Buck Johnson?"

Miss May nodded slowly. "We're friends of his. Did you know him?"

"I did know Buck. He was a terrific chef."

"Did you like him?" asked Miss May.

Jeffrey flashed a pained smile. "Sure. Great guy. I'm sorry, is there a point to these questions?"

Jeffrey shifted his weight from one foot to the other, then shoved his hands in his pockets. *Hmmm. Why was the owner of Hudgen's getting fidgety all of a sudden?*

"I take it you haven't heard the news," said Miss May with solemnity.

Jeffrey shook his head. "News?"

"Buck Johnson died this past weekend."

"Oh." Jeffrey lowered his head. "What a terrible thing to hear. I'm not looking forward to sharing that news with my staff. Some of them knew Buck well. Do you mind me asking what the cause of death was?"

Miss May pursed her lips. "Looks like a heart attack, maybe. But no one really knows."

"More depressing news in the culinary community," said Jeffrey. "I'm not sure if the three of you are aware, but restauranteurs, chefs, so many of us in the restaurant industry have a reputation for living hard and fast. It's not uncommon for us to die young. I've tried to stave that off with running five miles a day and a mostly healthy diet but it can happen to anyone. I'm sorry. I'm blathering. I'm just... I'm shocked. Please allow me to bring out a complimentary crème brûlée."

"That's fine," said Miss May. "We're stuffed, really."

"I insist. For friends of Buck."

Jeffrey gave us a polite nod and then hurried back to the kitchen. The crème brûlée arrived a few minutes later, and it was transcendent. But I barely ate a bite. Miss May, Teeny, and I were too busy having a hushed discussion about our conversation with Jeffrey.

None of us trusted that his reaction to Buck's death was genuine. Nor could we shake the image of all those perfect little bottles in the apothecary, with their strange and witchy ingredients.

Cassava. I knew I had seen it in Rebecca's shop too, and something about it bothered me. I vowed to Google it later, since Googling at the dinner table was rude even during a murder investigation.

In the meantime, all I could do was speculate and wonder...*did those special potions for better sleep and fewer wrinkles have a deadly side effect? And what was up with Hudgen's restaurant and their nervous owner?*

35

NINJA TURTLE

*W*e got home late that night. Way too late to locate Rebecca or to do much productive research on Hudgens or Cassava. So I cuddled up with a good mystery and a cup of hot cocoa by the fireplace.

That particular evening, I cracked open my worn copy of Agatha Christie's *The Body in the Library*. Reading Agatha Christie mysteries always gave me a warm, comfortable feeling, like I was getting a hug for the duration of the book. There was something soothing about British people and their manners, even when they were murdering each other.

I thought of Teeny and her obsession with *Jenna and Mr. Flowers* and other BBC mysteries and assumed she felt the same way. British accents were so soft and friendly, they could discuss a stabbing with the utmost gentility. I wondered, *did British people feel that way about their own voices?* I made a mental note to ask the next British person I encountered. Although I figured that might be a while, since I lived in a small town in upstate New York.

Miss May had gone to bed early so I had the entire first floor of the house to myself. Everything was so quiet I was able to get deep into the book in just a few minutes. But after an hour or two of peaceful reading, a knock at the back door startled me.

I placed the book down on the coffee table, pulled the knitted blanket from my lap and got to my feet. For a moment, I stood there listening, to see if the knock would come again. There was quiet for a few seconds. But then...

Knock, knock, knock.

I padded into the kitchen and spotted a silhouette standing on the back porch. I gulped. *What if it was the killer?* Odd for them to knock, but hey, maybe they were British and too polite to break and enter.

I looked around for a potential weapon. I settled on a wooden spoon from near the stove and brandished it like a sword. "Hello? Who's there?"

"Oh sweet mellifluous sound," a man responded. "How I've longed to hear the dulcet tones of your voice, placid like the surface of the Caspian Sea on a day with no wind."

I smiled. "Germany Turtle."

I swung open the door and there stood my lion-loving boyfriend, still dressed head to toe in his khaki safari gear from Africa.

"Hello," he said with a slight bow. "Has it been years since I last saw you, or does it simply feel that way?"

I pulled Germany close and kissed him as I laughed.

He kissed me back and pulled away. "You have more beauty in a single fingertip than can be found on the entire continent of Africa and beyond. Your eyes sparkle more brightly than every diamond. Your hair cascades with more wonder than all the waterfalls combined. And your skin is smoother than the sands of the Sahara."

"Yeah, yeah," I said. "You look good too. Come in! Why didn't you tell me you were coming?"

Germany turned up his hands. "You know I am a man who loves surprises."

I gave Germany another hug and then took his face in my hands. "Looks like you got a lot of sun," I said. "Like, a lot, a lot! I like it. Makes your eyes pop." I opened the refrigerator and looked at the contents. "You must be hungry. Let me see what I have. Apple pie, of course. Appie Oaters, you love those. There's leftover pizza in here, too."

Germany perked up. "Pizza sounds great. The food in Africa has been very rice and bean oriented. And there's been a lot of interesting game. I've dreamt many nights about devouring a slice of New York pizza."

"Do you want me to heat it up?"

"Cold is even better," said Germany.

He took a big bite of pizza and closed his eyes in ecstasy. "Nowhere else in the world is this delicacy available. You couldn't have prepared a more perfect food for me if you tried. Thank you."

I sat down across from Germany. "So talk to me. How are the lions? How long you here for? What's going on?"

"The lions are terrific. We've begun to understand their lifestyle more and more deeply with each passing day. One of the lion cubs, I call him Andrew, has taken a liking to me. But I'm afraid if we get too close, his mother will eat me so I keep my distance. He's adorable though, you would love him."

Kitty hopped up on a kitchen chair and looked at Germany. "Hi there, Kitty. Did you know we were talking about cats?" Germany grinned. "Don't worry. You're still the cutest."

"Oh she knows," I said.

I ruffled Kitty's scruff and she purred. I asked Germany several more questions about his time in Africa but he held up his hand to stop me before I finished. "Chelsea. I'm going to answer all your questions. Nothing will delight me more. But first I have something to tell you."

I took a closer look at Germany. He had an unfamiliar expression on his face. His mouth was tight and his brows were furrowed. And it didn't make me feel good. "What's going on?" I asked.

"I'll tell you what's going on," said Germany. "I journeyed back in my adopted hometown of Pine Grove because I missed everything about this place, of course. But more than that I've been plagued by lonely, empty nights far away from you. On those nights I have found my mind wandering, thinking about you and our possible future together. I'm not here tonight to make any grand gestures or ask any big questions, so you can relax your shoulders." I did as I was told. "But I want you to know that I have returned on this particular date in October because I wanted to be back home for Fall Fest. I know you love Fall Fest, getting your face painted, drinking pumpkin spiced everything, jumping around in big piles of hay..." *I've never jumped in hay. It did sound fun, though.* "So I think Fall Fest is the perfect occasion for us to discuss the nature of our relationship. And our future together."

Germany took a bite of pizza, like he hadn't just invited a very large elephant into the room. My mouth went dry. I hadn't seen the guy in what felt like forever and suddenly there he was, a few feet away from me, eating pizza and talking about the rest of our lives together.

Was Germany going to propose to me at Fall Fest? What was I going to say? How long was he going to chew that bite of pizza?

Germany swallowed. "You are planning on attending Fall Fest, correct?"

I nodded. "Good. Sunday afternoon, is that right?"

"That's right."

"Terrific. I'd love to spend every minute with you until then, if possible."

I looked down. "Of course. Me too. Um, but we're kind of in the middle of a big murder investigation. I'm not sure if I'm going to be around that much. But I want to see you, of course. You're here from Africa! So I'll definitely see you at Fall Fest, if not before."

"Blood runs in the streets of Pine Grove, yet again," said Germany. "We're all lucky to have you, Teeny, and Miss May to fight for justice. And I suppose we're unlucky that murderers keep choosing our town to practice their evil craft. What was the nature of this particular crime?"

I sighed. "Poisoned cinnamon bun."

"Any suspects?"

"A few." I took a bite of Germany's crust and my mind turned back to our case. I remembered my intention to Google 'cassava.' Sometimes Germany, with his massive vocabulary and strange pockets of knowledge, was sort of like a human Google...so I asked him instead of my phone. "Hey Germany...there's cassava root in Africa, right?"

"Oh yes," Germany said with a vigorous nod. "Cassava this, cassava that. It's like potatoes in America."

"Is it good for you?"

"Sort of," said Germany. "But only when you prepare it right. It naturally contains cyanide, so you have to be careful."

I gulped. Cyanide. The poison used to kill Buck Johnson.

36

DEAD ON ARRIVAL

*T*eeny, Miss May, and I arrived at Rebecca's little house in Blue Mountain early the next morning armed with a fresh apple pie and our steeliest resolves. But when I saw the scene at Rebecca's house I dropped the pie and my resolve went with it.

Cops were everywhere. The house was cordoned off with police tape. An ambulance was parked out front and I could see several EMTs in the house, through the open front door.

"Oh no," said Miss May. "Something happened to Rebecca."

"Let's talk to the cops. I bet Wayne and Flanagan are in there." I took two steps toward the house and Miss May grabbed my arm to stop me.

"Wait. They don't know we're here yet. Let's observe and see what we can learn."

"Maybe everything's OK," said Teeny. "Maybe Rebecca just set off the smoke alarm in her kitchen or something. That happens all the time. I set off the smoke alarm at the restaurant and the department shows up with four firetrucks."

"How many ambulances do they bring?" I asked.

"Shoot. Forget about the ambulance." Teeny looked around. "There also aren't any firetrucks here."

Another cop car pulled up in front of the house and a few young deputies spilled out. That made a total of six police squad cars at the scene of the crime. That was six more cop cars than I ever wanted to see at the home of a potential suspect.

"You two see the EMTs inside?" Miss May asked.

I took a breath and let it out. "Yeah. Looks like three or four of them are in the living room. Should we try to circle the house and get a look in the other rooms?"

Miss May shook her head. "Too many cops. We don't want to be seen prowling around like that. Whatever happened in there is not good."

"Hold on a second." Teeny cupped her hands on her forehead and peered toward the house. "Every single one of those cop cars is from Pine Grove. That doesn't make any sense. We're in Blue Mountain."

"Blue Mountain is basically a hamlet of Pine Grove," said Miss May. "They don't have their own police or fire so Pine Grove police cover most of the activity here."

"Oh yeah," said Teeny. "I knew that. Man sometimes I wish I could remember everything I know. If I knew all the things that I know I'd be brilliant, for sure."

Miss May gestured toward the house. "Flanagan and Wayne seem very interested in that girl over there. Do either of you recognize her?"

I took another look in that direction. Sure enough, Chief Flanagan and Wayne were questioning a Hispanic girl who looked to be in her 20's. The girl had shiny hair and big, brown eyes. She was rubbing her temples and her jaw was set tight.

"I don't know her," I said.

"Me neither," said Teeny. "Seems like maybe she's the one who found the body."

"I was thinking the same thing," I said. "No matter what the crime scene is like, the cops are always most focused on the person who discovers the victim, at least to start. And I don't see any other people here. No witnesses or anything."

"Backup," said Miss May. "We don't even know if there's a body that needed to be found. This could have been any kind of crime. Maybe Rebecca's house was broken into. Maybe Rebecca had a psychotic break. Maybe–"

The EMTs emerged from the home carrying a stretcher. There was a body on the stretcher, covered by a crisp, white sheet.

Miss May slumped. "I was wrong. There's a body."

"Rebecca," I said. "Poor woman."

Miss May headed toward the house. "Let's see if we can overhear anything helpful."

Seconds later, we were huddled up against the police tape, listening. Miss May and Teeny kept their ears tuned in to the police officers who were scattered about Rebecca's lawn. I watched as the EMTs loaded the body into the ambulance. The sheet slipped off as they loaded the gurney up. A burly EMT quickly replaced the sheet, but he wasn't quick enough. I saw that it was Rebecca. And she was dead.

Flanagan wrapped up her interview with the Hispanic girl and charged toward us. "I see you there, ladies! This is a crime scene. Vacate the premises. Now."

"We're standing on the street, on the pedestrian side of police tape," said Miss May. "We're not doing anything wrong. So I don't think we're going to leave, thank you."

"So you're going to disobey police orders?" Flanagan reached toward her handcuffs. "OK. I guess you're in the mood for jail food tonight. What's on the menu? I think it's crackers. Actually, who cares what it is? You're getting nothing but crackers."

"We're trying to help," I said. "That girl over there... Is she the one who found the body?"

"I will not disclose that information." Flanagan turned and called out to Deputy Hercules, just as skinny and acne-ridden as the day I met him. "Hercules. Can you escort these ladies off the premises?"

"Yes, chief."

"Wait," said Miss May. "Tell us what happened. You know that we're going to find out soon enough. Please."

Hercules ducked under the police tape and stood beside us with his chest puffed. "Ready to go, ladies?"

"Don't talk to us in that fake deep voice," said Teeny. "We all know you still squeak when you talk.

"Go home," said Flanagan. "I don't want to see you poking around this house any more today. Or ever. Any crimes that need to be solved will be solved by the Pine Grove Police Department. You can trust me on that. Have a nice day."

Flanagan strode back toward Wayne, her beautiful, soft red hair blowing in the wind. I cursed her beauty under my breath. Then I cursed the overall incompetence of the Pine Grove Police Department. I had little confidence they were going to solve this crime or any other.

And that meant Teeny, Miss May, and I had a lot of work to do.

37

COFFEE BREAK

*A*s soon as we entered the Brown Cow, the owner, Brian, welcomed us with a big, glowing smile. The charming local coffee shop was one of our favorite spots in Pine Grove, due at least in some part to that easy smile. And seeing Brian gladdened me, despite having just left the scene of a murder.

"Welcome, ladies," said Brian. "I'm in an extra good mood today. And I'm thrilled to see you!"

"Why is that?" I asked.

"I came into a little cash. Finally had the money to fix my espresso machine! That puppy's barking loud and clear today and I'm loving every drink she turns out!"

"Congrats," I said. "Business has been good?"

"You could say that," said Brian. "Plus, don't you just love October? Great, crisp weather all month. Then when it starts to get cold you're rewarded with Halloween. I can't wait for Halloween. What is it, 20 days away? I already have my costume. I'm going to be a bumblebee. I know, not that original, but I love bees. So if you don't like it, I don't want to hear it."

"Let me guess," I said. "You've already had a few cups of coffee?"

Brian laughed. "What gave it away?"

"I think your costume sounds great," said Miss May. "Can I please have a caramel latte? Extra caramel, extra foam, double espresso?"

"Same for me," said Teeny. "But I barely want any espresso and toss a few handfuls of chocolate sprinkles on mine if you can."

"I'll have the closest thing you've got to a caffeinated milkshake," I said.

"Coming right up." Brian turned away to start making the drinks but he kept the conversation going. "So what's going on? You three seem...lost in thought."

"You've got that right," said Miss May. "We're thinking."

"I see," said Brian. "Why don't you take the big table in the back by the window? That way you can think as much as you need and no suspicious characters will be nearby to eavesdrop. And drinks are on me today, OK? It's the least I can do to help you solve this case."

Miss May sighed. "Everyone's treating me to free stuff lately. First I didn't like it. Now I'm getting too used to it. Thank you, Brian."

Teeny and I echoed Miss May's gratitude, then we took a seat at the table Brian had suggested.

"I can't believe Rebecca is dead," I said. "Now, even if she did poison Buck, we'll never get to talk to her about it."

"I think Rebecca's death proves her innocence in the murder of Buck Johnson," said Miss May. "My gut tells me Rebecca knew something about Buck's death so Buck's killer took her out. That's depressing, for sure. But the silver lining is that our chances of solving this murder just doubled."

"How?" said Teeny.

"Two victims means two crimes. Twice as many chances for mistakes. Maybe the bad guy had less time to plan Rebecca's murder and got sloppy. I don't know," Miss May conceded. "But I'm trying to remain hopeful."

Brian approached our table. "Extra caffeine, extra sprinkles, and pretty much a milkshake. Let me know if you need anything else."

As Brian walked away, I leaned back in my comfy, overstuffed armchair and let out a small sigh of relief. I reflected on how lucky I was to live in a place where the business owners knew me and respected me and didn't laugh when I ordered a milkshake for my morning coffee.

When I looked around the coffee shop at all the comfortable furniture and the happy customers, I felt a renewed sense of confidence in our ability to solve the case. Although Rebecca's death was a setback, we'd handled worse before. And in the cocoon of community that Pine Grove provided, I knew I could find the strength and wisdom needed to find the poisoner of the smoking bun.

"Rebecca's death is upsetting," I said, sitting up tall. "We can all agree on that. But it doesn't matter if there are twice as many clues or half as many clues. Because what we do is solve murders in this town. We keep the streets and the people safe. We defend their sense of justice and fairness in the world. Kids growing up in Pine Grove need to understand that bad guys get punished, and good guys can live in security and comfort. We all need that. So let's talk suspects and quit moping around."

Miss May and Teeny exchanged glances, their necks swinging toward one another like they were prairie dogs scoping out the flatlands.

"Wow. That caffeine must be kicking in quick. I don't

think I've ever heard such an impassioned speech out of you," said Miss May. "I liked it."

"It scared me," said Teeny. "Angry Chelsea is scary Chelsea. I wouldn't want to be on the other side of that."

"Let's talk about that girl who found Rebecca's body," I said. "I didn't recognize her at all, so everything about her is suspicious to me. First of all, it didn't appear she was related to Rebecca, so I don't understand why she was at Rebecca's house so early in the morning. Could she have been a rival apothecary owner? Good question. I don't know but I want to find out. Or maybe she was a disgruntled customer. Or a neighbor or someone from Rebecca's past who wanted her dead."

"Those are all great theories." Teeny took a huge sip of her drink and when she lowered the cup, she had whipped cream and sprinkles all over her upper lip. "So let's go get her. Interrogate her. Miss May and I will be the good cops. Chelsea, you'll be the bad cop. Keep up this energy. I like it. And after this case is solved, we'll find you a softball team to coach. Those girls need you. They need someone who believes in them. We can win big this year if we try."

"Why are you talking about softball?" Miss May asked.

"I don't know. I got caught up," said Teeny.

"Hang on a second," I said. "Teeny, thank you for your confidence in my coaching ability. I'm not looking for any extra commitments right now but I'm sure I could take any group of girls, no matter how ragtag they are, and dominate in states this year. I'm going to keep that in mind. But we're not done talking about suspects."

"I thought we decided to find out more about the girl who found the body," said Miss May.

"We decided she was suspicious and we should consider it," I said. "But I think we need to spend a little more time with Hannah. She's squirrelly. Normally, I like squirrels. But not when the squirrels come in human form. Then I don't trust them."

"You lost me," said Teeny. "What's wrong with squirrels?"

"Forget the squirrel thing. What I'm saying is that as far as I can see, Hannah remains our chief suspect. I think she found out Buck was cheating on her so she flipped out and killed him. Then, when that level of vengeance didn't feel good enough, she found Buck's lover, Rebecca, and killed her as well."

"I don't want to kill your buzz," said Miss May. "But why would Hannah wait to commit these murders so long after her separation with Buck?"

"Because she's a woman," I said. "No offense to any of us but sometimes we try to be OK with something and we try to be peaceful and put something out of our mind and then, one day, we snap."

Teeny pointed at me. "She's right. I do that. I do it all the time. Once I wrote a horrible online review for someone who cut my hair six years after the bad haircut. For that whole time I told myself I was going to rise above it and I didn't want to put her down in public. Then one day I went for it. And I said some nasty things, all deserved, mind you. Some might say the review was vicious but twenty-one people voted it as 'funny,' which I like."

"So you want to talk to Hannah?" asked Miss May.

I set my jaw and looked out the window with a determined look in my eye. "As soon as I finish my milkshake."

38

BAD TO THE BONE

*O*ne thing I had learned since moving back to Pine Grove was that murder was bad for business.

Something about a dead body works like a force field against paying customers. I always wondered, *did people believe the buildings were haunted? Or was it a general fear of death that kept visitors at bay?*

Even regulars stayed away after a murder. Miss May and I had learned that firsthand at the orchard and in the bakeshop. Sometimes catching the killer helped revitalize the business. But even then, there was a tainted quality that could linger for weeks, even months. Hard to pin down the reason for something so intangible but it was real as a thunderstorm on a summer afternoon.

Regardless of the reason, there wasn't a single customer at *Peter's Land and Sea* the morning of Rebecca's death. The place had been so busy just a week prior, the rapid downturn shocked me.

When Hannah saw us from her post behind the hostess stand, she closed her eyes for a few seconds, then reopened them and spoke with great calm. "Go away. Please. No one here has anything to say to you. And we don't need you poking around the business today. If you want to look around this place, go to the police academy, pass the physical, attend the classes, become an officer, and come back next year.

"Well that's the thing," said Miss May, "the reason we poke around, as you put it, is that police officers don't do such a good job. The people of Pine Grove need us amateur sleuths to get to the truth when the cops can't."

"You really believe that," said Hannah. "It's amazing how power affects people's brains."

"We don't have any power, that's the point," said Miss May. "We're not interested in titles, quotas or promotions. All we want is the truth."

"The truth? OK. The truth is, Chief Flanagan told me that if you came back here she would arrest you, no questions asked. And she says she'd be happy to charge all three of you with any number of crimes that she knows will stick. Harassment, trespassing, pick your poison."

"Interesting choice of words," Teeny muttered.

"What was that?" Hannah snapped.

"I didn't say anything," said Teeny.

"We'll go," I said, drawing on the strength and support of my imaginary softball coaching job, "if you agree to answer one question with a hundred percent honesty."

"Fine," Hannah snorted. "What?"

"Did you know that Buck and Rebecca were having an affair?"

Hannah laughed. "That's what this is about. You think I killed Rebecca because I'm a jealous wife."

I looked over at Miss May. She shrugged. It appeared neither of us knew what was so funny. "Something like that," I said.

Hannah shook her head. "Buck and I didn't have nearly such an old-fashioned relationship."

"You mean..." Teeny began. "You weren't always, uh, monogamous?"

"That's right. We had what the kids call an 'open relationship.' Buck was allowed to have all the fun he wanted with any girl he liked. It never bothered me. And the same was true in the opposite direction. See, I'm what you call a true feminist? I never allowed a man to possess me and I've never expected to possess a man. That's not to say the men and women with whom we sometimes had relations couldn't get possessive. Some of Buck's girlfriends were very possessive, in fact. If I were you, I would talk to some of them."

"Excuse us for a second." I pulled Miss May away and turned my back to Hannah so she wouldn't hear me speak. "The woman who found Rebecca's body must have been one of Buck's girlfriends."

"Seems likely," said Miss May. "That girl also had brown hair. Just like the hair we saw in the brush."

Hannah cleared her throat. "Anything you have to say you can say in front of me. I'm being honest with you and I expect the same in return."

"Sorry. I was just telling Miss May that I have a doctor's appointment later and I didn't want to forget. It's a serious medical issue. Pinky toe problems. Everyone says you don't need those little guys but let me tell you... You do. I hope I don't have to get mine amputated. But something is definitely up with it. The left one. Maybe a fungus?"

Hannah curled her lip. "That's disgusting. Stop talking about your pinky toe fungus."

"Sorry. I'm just...nervous. About amputation. I mean, if

it's not a fungus... maybe it's gangrene. Gout? Who knows? I'm just theorizing. I'll stop."

"OK, Chelsea," said Teeny. "That's good. You've got a funky pinky toe. Let's get back to this open relationship thing. Did that really work?"

"Sure," said Hannah. "Until it didn't. But plenty of 'closed' relationships don't work either."

"I could never do it," said Teeny. "It's hard enough managing one relationship. And men are so annoying. Listen, I'm lucky I found Big Dan. He's great. But there's only one of him. How do you even find enough guys you like? I mean, most of 'em are smelly deadbeats, you know?"

"I managed," Hannah said. "Now if you'll excuse me, I need to get back to work."

I looked around at the empty restaurant. I couldn't imagine we were keeping Hannah from anything important.

"One more question," said Miss May.

Hannah crossed her arms. "Quickly, please. I'm busy."

"If you were fine with Buck seeing other women..." Miss May began. "Can I ask... Why did you separate?"

Hannah threw up her hands. "Why does anyone separate? We were bored with each other. We stopped making each other laugh. I had begun to dread kissing him good night or giving him a hug in the morning. And the sight of his beer belly somehow transformed from a cute feature to a hideous paunch I abhorred."

Miss May turned down the sides of her mouth. "OK. You are being honest."

"You've never been there in a relationship?" Hannah asked. "Where you just... don't see what you saw before?"

"I have." Teeny raised her hand. "I've been there in lots of relationships. Possibly every relationship I've ever had ended with me hating the sight of some guy's gut. Well, that and I had an unfortunate attraction to magicians for a while that just didn't work out."

"Great," said Hannah. "And Chelsea, I heard you haven't always been lucky in love, either."

"I was left at the altar so, yeah, you could say that was unlucky. And my fiancé stole my whole business. And he broke my heart like a piece of wood over his knee in karate class. But you know. I'm over it."

"See?" said Hannah. "I'm just a woman like all three of you. You may not believe this, but Buck's death hasn't been easy on me. Yeah, we had started to bother each other in a million little ways. And big ones. But a lot of love remained between us and I miss him."

I could tell Hannah was telling the truth. But I still didn't know if we could trust her. Still, there wasn't much more to say, so the three of us trudged back to the truck with our heads hung low. Had we pushed Hannah too far? Or had we not gone far enough? Hard to say and I wasn't sure we'd ever find out.

Petey caught up to us just before we climbed into the truck. "Chelsea! Miss May! Hold up!"

We turned back. Miss May scrunched up her nose. "Petey. How can we help you?"

"I heard what you all were talking about with Hannah."

"OK..." Miss May said.

"She was telling the truth. Hannah and Buck had an open relationship. Wide open. That thing was like the Grand Canyon. Buck was slimy about it, for sure. He was always hitting on the waitresses here. But Hannah was never bothered by Buck's affairs."

"Why are you telling us this?" I asked.

"I don't know. I thought it might help." Petey sighed. "If

you don't find this killer soon, I'm going to go out of business."

Miss May put her hand on Petey's elbow. "I know how that goes. But don't worry. We'll find the bad guy and people will come back. I promise."

Petey nodded and returned to the restaurant. I watched him go and couldn't help but wonder...

Would Miss May be able to keep that promise? Or would this killer disappear and take Petey's successful business with them?

39

OPEN AND SHUT

*W*e went to *Grandma's* to grab a quick lunch and discuss our conversation with Hannah.

We arrived at the restaurant and Teeny's mom, Granny, was sitting on her normal stool, fast asleep with her chin on her chest.

"How does your mom sleep while sitting on a stool?" I asked.

"She has a strong core. All the doctors tell her. The woman has a four pack and she's like a million years old."

"I don't have any packs and I'm less than a quarter of that age," I said. "What's her workout secret?"

Teeny shook her head. "No idea. Maybe she developed the muscles from all these years sleeping upright in the stool."

"I do chair yoga," said Teeny's mom, blinking herself awake and sitting up in the stool. "I've told you, Teeny, chair yoga is the answer to all your exercise needs."

"I walked all the way from the orchard to the restaurant a few days ago," said Miss May.

"Let's see your abs," said the little old lady.

"I'm going to need a lot of time or a lot of surgery before anybody sees anything like abs," said Miss May.

"OK, Mama. We're working on a case. Go back to sleep. Or you know, maybe do something to run the restaurant." Granny waved Teeny off, and Teeny bounced away like a teenage girl after talking to her mom. "Come on. Let's grab our booth."

I smiled as I followed Teeny. It was nice to think of her as a teenager, bopping around Pine Grove with her signature blonde hair. The thought of it made me forget the murders for a second. But only for a second.

"Alright," I said as soon as we sat. "Let's talk about this open relationship thing."

"I don't know if it's gonna work for you and Germany," Teeny said. "And Wayne doesn't seem like he'd love it either."

"I don't want an open relationship," I said. "I'm talking about Buck, Hannah and Rebecca. Remember? The dead guy, his wife and his recently deceased lover?"

"Right," said Teeny. "But hold on! First, I've got a new menu item that I need the two of you to try."

I scanned the menu but didn't see anything. Miss May did the same then looked up and shrugged. "I'm stumped. What did you add?"

"Look at the very bottom."

I traced my finger all the way to the bottom of the menu and there I found a listing for the new item. A lobster roll with truffle oil and "fancy mushrooms."

I shook my head. "Teeny. You're still trying to compete with *Land and Sea* in the gourmet food market? *Grandma's* isn't that kind of place. And Petey's is suffering. The chef who stole your hashbrown lasagna is dead."

"So what? That doesn't mean I can't be better than him!"

Teeny flagged down a waiter. "Two of the lobster, truffle, mushroom things please."

"Where did you get the lobster?" Miss May asked.

"Don't worry about it," said Teeny. "It's fresh and delicious."

"I also see here that the lobster roll is served with something called 'fancy' mushrooms," said Miss May. "What do you mean by 'fancy?'"

"They're fancy. I don't know. They all had long, confusing, fancy names. I don't have room for all those names on the menu so I wrote fancy. Do you not know what fancy means? Fine, forget it. I'll cancel the lobster rolls. Is that what you want?"

"No," said Miss May with widened eyes, "it's fine. I'm sorry for questioning your food. I'm looking forward to it."

"Good." Teeny fidgeted with the silverware in front of her. "Now we can talk about the open relationship thing. And I have to say, I'm a bit of an expert on this topic."

"Don't tell me," said Miss May, "you learned about open relationships on *Jenna and Mr. Flowers*."

Teeny looks disgusted. "Of course not. *Jenna and Mr. Flowers* is a polite British show. It's sweet and clean and monogamous to its core. I learned about open relationships on *The North Port Diaries*."

I laughed. "I haven't heard you mention that show in forever. Wow. You used to love it."

"I still love it. But I can love other shows, too. I have an open relationship with my mystery series, that's all. Anyway, in *North Port Diaries* every single relationship is open. The people in town insist that they can handle the complications. They all say that they're so attractive they deserve as many significant others as they can handle. But let me tell you... That system is flawed. It just doesn't work out. And it often leads to murder, intrigue, mystery, suspicion, all that juicy stuff."

"So you think Hannah was lying to us," I said. "You think the open relationship was a problem."

"No," said Teeny. "Seems like she was being honest about all that. Plus, Petey backed her up and that kid can't lie to save his life."

"Petey lied to us earlier in this investigation about firing Buck," said Miss May.

"OK, fine," Teeny said. "But that was more of an omission. And he wasn't lying this time. I could tell."

"So what's your theory?" I asked.

"It's obvious." Teeny filled our water glasses from a pitcher on the table. "Hannah didn't get jealous and snap. The other girlfriend did. The girl who 'found' Rebecca's body. Seems to me that girl murdered Buck, probably because Buck had even more girlfriends. And then she murdered Rebecca. She seemed like a cinnamon bun baker to me. Cute but deadly."

"That all seems like it could be true," I said. "But we don't know anything about that girl. Flanagan wouldn't even tell us her name. Plus, she's not from around here, so she could be anywhere now. What if she drove down twice a week from Massachusetts for a fling with Buck Johnson? People do crazy stuff like that. Affairs make them feel alive. The more inconvenient, the better. And if that's the case, we're never going to find her."

"Since when are you an expert on affairs?" asked Miss May.

I blushed. "I'm not. But I'll admit, I've seen a few episodes of *The North Port Diaries*."

Teeny clapped her hands together in her energetic little golf claps. "I knew it. I can't believe you kept this from me!

We could've been watching together. Like people did for that dragon show. A watch party."

"Sure, that sounds great," I said. "But right now I'm wondering if either of you have an answer to our current problem. How are we going to find out the identity of that woman with nothing to go on?"

"You said it yourself," said Miss May. "The police have her information."

I narrowed my eyes. "So..."

Miss May grinned. "So it seems to me you need to visit everybody's favorite handsome detective."

40

THE DOGGONE TRUTH

I smiled.

Amy's dog grooming van was parked in front of the police department. A line of canine cops waited by the van to be groomed, accompanied by their appointed officers. And most of the dogs were wagging their official police tails.

I spotted a rotund, unkempt officer near the front of the line and had the somewhat unkind thought that Amy should take care of his grooming issues, too.

Amy's perky, official voice rang out from inside the van. "OK, Officer Spot. Now we're going to do your tummy. Roll over. Good boy! Here's a treat."

I laughed. It was nice to see that Amy had scored the business of the local police department. And I was looking forward to seeing well-groomed, preppy little cop dogs parading around Pine Grove, keeping the peace.

I had to awkwardly excuse my way through the line of police officers on my way into the station. But Amy caught up to me before I went inside. "Chelsea, hey. How's Steve the dog? Are you happy with his cut?"

"Ecstatic," I said. "You transformed Steve from tramp to champ."

"That's my job!" She leaned in and spoke in a conspiratorial whisper. "What's going on with the case? Are you here to sleuth out some police secrets? I've been talking to these officers and their dogs all day. I swear some of the pups are smarter than the cops."

"Have you heard anyone discussing a possible murder in Blue Mountain?"

Amy shook her head. "Nope. But I'll keep my ears peeled. I think all the time I spend working with dogs has given me dog-like hearing, for what it's worth. And I have catlike reflexes. Next time I see you, remind me to tell you about the time I caught someone stealing a breastmilk pump out of my friend's car. Who steals a breastmilk pump? Turns out there's a big secondhand market for new mothers. Baby stuff is so expensive, I get it. But you can't steal one from a new mom herself. Then what? She goes to pump and she's stuck with no options? Not cool. Anyway, good luck in there."

Amy bustled away as quickly as she'd appeared and I laughed as I heard her addressing the next dog, Officer Rover. As I entered the police station, I wondered if she was talking to the dog or the man...

Wayne was working the front desk on that day. I don't know if it was the light, or his perfect level of stubble, but his jawline was looking extra strong. When he glanced up at me his blue-green eyes seemed two shades brighter than usual, like they were staring right through me. I froze in the x-ray beam of his eye contact for what felt like the entirety of "I Will Always Love You," by Whitney Houston. Then I heard a dog barking outside and snapped back to reality. "Wayne. Hey. Cool shirt."

Wayne looked down. "This is my standard issue police shirt."

"Yeah. It's cool. I've always thought it. They should sell those in the store. I bet they'd fly off the shelves. Like how snowbirds fly out of New York and head to Florida in the winter. Is your grandma still with us?"

Chelsea. Stop talking. Get a grip. Why are you bringing up grandmothers!?

"She is, actually," said Wayne with a little smile. "As a matter of fact, she's down in Boca. Spends most of her time on the shuffleboard court. I think she hustles people for cash, she's a real shark. Either that, or she's going on dates. Some swinging singles scene down there. I don't know how she has the energy. Sleeps five hours a night, at most. Jogs every morning. Incredible woman. I hope I'm like her one day."

"Going on lots of dates?" I couldn't keep my inner flirt contained. I blushed. *Did I just embarrass myself?*

"There's only one girl I want to date."

Was it possible that Wayne's gaze was actually burning a hole in my face?

"Right. Uh, well that's not why I'm here... To talk about dating. I can't talk about any of that right now. I'm here because I need a favor. Do you have a break coming up or anything?"

Wayne checked his watch. "I could take one right now."

Wayne and I exited the police station and walked toward the ice cream shop across the street. Wayne ordered a milkshake, but I was still full from my coffee milkshake earlier. So I asked for a literal cherry with a little laugh. The proprietor, Emily, generously gave me two.

Then Wayne and I sat at one of the tables and talked.

"So what's up?" Wayne asked.

"Um..." I was about to launch into my question about the identity of the girl that found Rebecca's body. But I spotted a mischievous glimmer in Wayne's eyes and decided I needed to be more tactful. It would be a bad idea to jump right into a discussion of the mysterious girl without a little small talk to ease into the conversation.

"Um what?" asked Wayne.

"Sorry. I forgot what I was going to say." I let out a throaty, guttural chuckle in my nervousness. It sounded to me like a distant, unattractive cousin of the girlish giggle. And Wayne looked confused.

"Are you OK, Chelsea?"

Honestly, no. I had started to sweat profusely and it wasn't a good look. But I didn't say that. Instead, I nodded like a bobblehead doll on a bumpy road.

"Look, I heard Germany's back in town..." Wayne said. "Is that why you're here? You want to talk about that?"

"Yes," I lied, grateful for a conversational escape hatch. "Um... You're my closest guy friend and I thought maybe you could give me some advice." As the words exited my mouth I cringed.

What was I doing? Did I actually think this age-old tactic would work on Wayne? And had I really just called him my 'guy friend?'

Wayne leaned forward. "Hey. I'm always here to talk."

Oh my goodness, it worked! ...which meant I was going to have to say more things. "Thank you. Well, Germany's back in town, which has been nice. But I've been running all over the place trying to figure out what happened to Buck and Rebecca. And I feel like I haven't gotten to spend enough time with him."

"You're struggling with work-life balance," said Wayne. "I listened to a podcast all about that recently. I mean, it can't be easy, amateur sleuthing and a long distance relationship? Plus, you have your real job at the orchard. That's a lot to juggle."

I nodded. "Yes. Uh-huh. True."

"Look, I'm sorry I was immature a few days ago when we were talking and Germany came up. You're a grown woman and you deserve to live whatever life you want. I don't care if you're dating Germany or me or the man on the moon. I want you to be happy. So... I'll try to help you with the investigation, if I can."

I looked up with my biggest doe eyes. "You would do that?"

Wayne looked around to make sure we were alone then he turned back to me with a sympathetic nod. "Of course. You're probably wondering about Rebecca, right? You want to know if she was murdered?"

"...yeah."

"Stop wondering. Trust your instincts."

"OK." I studied Wayne's face. Then I glanced down because my studies started to feel a little too...intimate.

Wayne took a sip of his milkshake. "Wow. This is good. You want to try?"

I shook my head. "No, thank you. But there's one thing that my instincts haven't told me that I'm hoping you could help me with?"

Wayne turned up his palms, as if to suggest that he would help if he could.

"The woman who found Rebecca's body... What's her name? Where does she live? None of us recognized her, which was weird."

"That I can't share," said Wayne. "But I'm sure you'll figure it out if you keep digging. The answer's out there."

"But time is important," I said. "And I'm not always a speedy digger."

"Legally, I can't tell you her name. If you overheard me discussing the fact that she shared a name with a certain famous *Disney* princess, I couldn't help that. But I couldn't confirm or deny anything."

"Ariel."

Wayne took a sip of his milkshake.

"Um. Belle. Cinderella. Tinkerbell."

Wayne kept sipping.

I gasped. "Jasmine."

Wayne smirked. Bullseye. Then he slid it across the table. "You should try this thing. It's incredible."

No one in the history of time has had to twist my arm to get me to take a sip of milkshake. Yes, I was full, but I couldn't resist.

Wayne was right. That milkshake was cold, creamy and delicious. It tasted like summer at the beach. I took a second sip, then slid it back.

"It looked like maybe Jasmine was from the city," I said. "She looked put together. Nice haircut. Expensive jeans. Are you allowed to tell me where she's from?"

Wayne shook his head. "I can't divulge any of that information. But I can tell you that my favorite pizza shop is in Brooklyn. Greenpoint, actually. Have you tried Paulie Gee's?"

I smirked. Wayne's code was inelegant and obvious but I supposed that somehow it must have protected his sense of legal duty to the police department, so I appreciated it.

"I haven't tried Paulie Gee's in Greenpoint, Brooklyn," I said. "But I'll add it to my list."

Wayne slurped up the last few sips of his milkshake and

looked up at me, eyes crinkled with a smile. "You wanna ask me any other questions?"

I shrugged. Wayne had provided the first name and hometown of the possible killer. That was more than I had expected. "I mean, I don't think I have any more questions. Why? Have you arrested someone or charged them for these murders?"

"I wasn't talking about those kinds of questions." Wayne leaned forward. He got closer and I got sweatier. "By the way..."

Was he going to try to kiss me? How was I going to handle that? What was I going to do? I'm not fit for open relationships!

Thankfully, Wayne spoke when he was mere inches from my face. "I've got news about the foot."

Wayne reclined back into his chair and chuckled. "You had no idea what I was going to say. You were freaking out. That was awesome."

I breathed a sigh of relief. "The foot. The severed foot. Of course."

What is my life? I wondered. *How am I in a place where news about a severed foot is somehow a relief to me?*

"What's the update?"

A smug look crossed Wayne's face. "We found a second foot. Outside of town, in an estuary. Must've been carried there from the brook on the orchard."

"What?!" I asked. "A second foot."

"That's right. And it matches the first foot. Same size, same shape, same hairy little toes. Pretty good development, I thought."

"I guess that's good. I mean, a foot washed right into your lap. And you still don't know whose foot it is. But—"

"Can you just be impressed, Chelsea? I'm trying to

impress you here! We found another foot. That's a hundred percent increase in the productivity of that investigation."

"OK. Sorry. Any clues about the owner of these feet?"

Wayne frowned. "No. No idea."

"Well let me know when you have an inkling," I said. "I need to plan a trip down to Brooklyn."

41

TWO LEFT FEET

"*He* actually told you something?" Miss May's eyes bugged out of her head.

"Yup. I was cunning and wise. And flirty."

Teeny smacked the table. "That's my girl. You used your feminine wiles to your advantage. We should do that more, come to think of it. We all have feminine wiles and we almost never use them."

"Yeah. We use our brains instead," said Miss May.

"If we were really using our brains we would use our feminine wiles," said Teeny. "That's objectively the smart thing to do. Men are more convinced by flirting than by thinking."

I shuddered. "Can we please stop saying wiles? It's giving me the creeps."

We were all gathered around the kitchen table at the farmhouse picking crumbs, and sometimes chunks, off of a little flatbread pizza Miss May had whipped up. The dough was thin and delicious. And the mozzarella was fresh from my favorite Italian deli. But both Teeny and Miss May had, perhaps not surprisingly, been more interested in my encounter with Wayne than by their dinner.

"You did good, Chelsea," said Miss May. "Maybe this is the beginning of a new chapter for us and the Pine Grove Police Department. Imagine if we can work in tandem with the police more often? Share information?"

"They can tell us anything they want," said Teeny. "But I don't think there's any need for us to return the favor. Not until they solve a couple murders on their own."

"That's just obstinate," said Miss May. "But I understand your point."

"What do you think we should do now?" Teeny asked. "We have Jasmine's first name. And we know she lives in Greenpoint. But Greenpoint is big. Are we just going to go there and start driving around with the windows down screaming the name 'Jasmine' as loud as we can?"

I smirked. "This is the moment where I can share my big, fun secret."

Teeny braced herself against the table. "Wayne tried to kiss you. You kissed him back. You took a moonlit walk along the Hudson and he told you about all his childhood fears. You confessed that you've loved him since the moment you set eyes on him and he said the same back to you. You're getting married in two years and the ceremony will be somewhere along the water in a nice river town. You want me and Miss May to make the wedding cake and you're going to name your firstborn daughter after me!"

"Uhhhhhh," I said. "What?!"

"It's not that much of a stretch," said Miss May. "Is that what happened?"

"I'm dating Germany!" I reminded them.

"But we all know you've got eyes for Wayne," said Miss May.

"Everybody has eyes for Wayne. He's a super-hot, smart, hunky, helpful, friendly man. Yeah, sometimes he stubborn or closed-off. But the same could be said for each one of us."

"So now you're defending him," said Teeny with a smile.

"I'm not defending him I'm just pointing out his character traits, good and bad."

"I would defend him too if I were in love with him," said Miss May.

"Oh my goodness! We didn't kiss! I stole his police pad!" I pulled a small yellow pad from my purse and slammed it down on the table. "There. Happy?"

Miss May picked up the police pad, squinted, and flipped a couple pages. "This handwriting is terrible. It looks like somebody put a pencil in his mouth and said, "Write me a sonnet.""

"OK. Fine. It's not the most legible handwriting I've ever seen. But look at the last page."

Miss May followed my instructions. She held the notebook close to her nose and squinted. "I can't tell what this says."

"Let me see," said Teeny.

Miss May handed Teeny the book. Teeny held it out at arm's length and tried to read the words. "I think it says, 'Hello flagpole. Sit in the garden box. Heavy rains expected, two to four inches.'"

I snatched the notebook back and pointed at the words as I spoke to them. "It says, 'Jasmine,' at the top of the page. That's the one word I can make out. And whatever's below it is formatted like an address. So it must be where she lives. If we can figure out how to read Wayne's handwriting it will take us right to our suspect."

"How are we ever going to figure out how to read that handwriting?" asked Teeny.

"I've got an idea," said Miss May. "But it'll have to wait 'til morning."

42

DOCTOR, DOCTOR, GIMME THE NEWS

*D*r. Ingles waiting room was old-fashioned and charming. It was also packed with people. A pair of toddlers played with colorful wooden blocks in the corner. A few elderly women sat in a row of chairs against the wall. And Miss May and I sat opposite one another, squeezed in between other waiting patients.

"How do you know this guy is going to be able to read Wayne's handwriting?" I asked.

"You wouldn't have to ask that if you'd ever seen Ingles' chicken scratch," said Miss May.

"So you think just because the doctor has bad handwriting, he's going to be able to read Wayne's handwriting? I don't know. I don't think the law of transposition applies to reading illegible scripts."

"Oh shove it," said Teeny. "Don't you talk big about your laws to us. We get it. You went to a fancy old college, maybe not Ivy League but there was plenty of ivy. They taught you all the laws. But this mission doesn't require college smarts. It requires street smarts and intuition. I agree with Miss

May. Ingles is going to be able to read this writing, no problem."

An elderly Asian woman stood up from her chair, crossed the room and sat next to Teeny. She leaned in to speak to us. "Are you three talking about your new investigation?"

"Hi, Janice," said Miss May. "No. We're just here because Ingles wrote a prescription and the pharmacist can't read it. So we had to come back to get the doctor to translate."

"Well I think Tom Gigley killed that cranky chef," Janice said.

Gigley hadn't come up in our investigation as a suspect. And I wondered what made this nice old woman so quick to accuse the erudite town lawyer of murder. "Why do you think that?"

"I've never liked that Gigley. Not one bit. The guy seems like a killer. And I hate his band."

Another elderly woman piped up from across the room, her voice thin and creaky. "Gigley did it. Is that what you're talking about?"

"That's right," Janice said.

"He's guilty for sure," said the other woman.

Janice turned back to us. "Me and all my friends, we hate Gigley together."

"Was he your lawyer at one point or something? Why do you hate him? Did he do a bad job? Or did he represent your husbands in a divorce, or...?"

"Never hired him," said Janice. "And I've never met him. But I hate his face. We all do."

The second woman chimed in once more from across the room. "I bet he killed Buck with a kitchen knife. One second, the poor guy was chopping an onion and the next second he was getting chopped!" The woman made a slicing motion around her neck with her finger. Then she let her head dramatically fall to one side and stuck her tongue out in an imitation of a dead person.

"What she said," said Janice. Then Janice repeated the throat slitting and head drooping motion, complete with stuck out tongue. I stifled a laugh.

"We'll take that into consideration," said Miss May. "Thank you."

Ten minutes later, Teeny, Miss May, and I were crowded into the exam room waiting for Dr. Ingles. The place looked like a classic doctor's office. There was a chart of the human body on the door, a couple of stiff vinyl chairs, a doctor's table, and a few framed diplomas on the wall.

The doctor entered with a big smile. He was tall and skinny and appeared to have been stretched out, like in a kid's cartoon. His face was long and bony but he had bright eyes and an energetic personality. "Ladies, greetings. Was I offering a three for one deal on physicals that I'm not aware of?"

"Actually, we're here because we were hoping you could help us with an investigation," said Miss May.

"Would you like me to investigate your health? Not a problem. Hop on the scale and we'll get going."

"No one is getting weighed here," said Teeny with a stern tone of voice. "I had a big breakfast and my shoes weigh at least three pounds. We're talking about a murder investigation."

Ingles eyebrows jumped halfway up his forehead. "Finally. I was wondering if the three of you would ever call on my expertise! Is there a piece of medical evidence you'd like me to assess?"

"Not quite," I said.

"Chelsea Rae Thomas," said Ingles, "How are you? You, I know for a fact, are overdue for a physical. It's been what, one or two years since your fiancé left you and you moved back into your childhood home? I haven't seen you once in that whole time. We want you in peak physical shape, especially if you're going to be out there karate kicking bad guys."

"I'll make an appointment with the receptionist on the way out," I said. "Anyway, we were wondering if you could read the handwriting on this note." I pulled Wayne's police pad from my purse, flipped to the correct page and handed it to the doctor.

Ingles read Wayne's horrific handwriting as though the note had been typed in twenty-point, bold font on a computer. "Sure. This is a name and address. Jasmine America, 25 Locksley Place, Greenpoint, Brooklyn, New York."

"I knew you were going to be able to read that horrible handwriting," said Miss May. "What a gift you have!"

"A lifetime of reading my own horrible handwriting, and that of my colleagues, has trained me well. I suspect I could decode hieroglyphics without any practice, too. Is there anything else you need me to read?"

"You don't have a crystal ball, do you?" Teeny asked. "We could use a little psychic assistance."

"I'm sad to say, I do not," said Ingles. "But even without a crystal ball, I know to tell the three of you to be careful out there. I heard another body was found. That means there's still a dangerous element in Pine Grove. And if the three of you are at all close to apprehending the villain, he or she might try to silence you before you uncover the truth."

There was a somber, quiet moment, then Ingles perked up. "OK. I want all three of you in here for a physical, preferably separate appointments, sometime in the next two months. Have a good one."

Ingles looked happy as he bounced away but I knew he was right to warn us. The killer might have it out for me, Teeny, or Miss May. And I was long overdue for my physical.

43

PICKING UP CLUES

We hopped into my pickup truck, jumped on the highway headed south toward New York City.

"First of all, why do those ladies suspect Tom Gigley of killing Buck?" asked Teeny. "Tom's idea of a sophisticated meal is Spam with Grey Poupon. I doubt he's ever even eaten at *Land and Sea* or been in the same room with Buck Johnson."

"I don't think any of us think Tom did it," I said. "Otherwise I wouldn't be driving to Greenpoint right now to try to find that Jasmine woman."

"Right," said Miss May, "if we suspected Tom, we would have walked to Tom's office to question him right now."

"Do you mean that?" Teeny said. "Because he's my friend. I'm not saying I haven't suspected him before, the guy has a temper, but I don't think he did this one."

"He didn't," I said. "That was just gossip."

"So those ladies hate him for no reason?" Teeny crossed her arms. "It's not fair. You can't go around hating people based on nothing."

"Those are bold words spoken by a woman who hates a lot of people," I said.

"I hate everybody for a reason. I mean, I don't hate everybody. But all the people I hate deserve to be hated. I don't just sit around in doctor's offices accusing the perfectly nice town lawyer of murder! I mean, what in the world? Tom is a friendly grump. A sourpuss with a sweet heart. He's one of my best customers at the restaurant. Three eggs, four slices of bacon, and a short stack of pancakes. And he always finishes everything except for a few bites of pancake."

"Yikes," I said. "It sounds like Tom is the one who might need to get a physical. He eats that every morning?"

"Hey. I thought this was a judgment free zone," said Teeny.

I kept my hands on ten and two. "You're right. No judgment. Everything's fine. I'm sure Tom is... healthy as a horse."

"This is a strange case," said Miss May. "I'm still thinking about Buck and Hannah's open relationship. We had assumed, if Hannah did it, her motive was jealousy. But if she knew about Buck's girlfriends and didn't care that means she doesn't have a motive anymore."

"It's possible she lied to us," I said. "Maybe she hated the open relationship all along."

"I didn't get that impression from Hannah," said Miss May.

"Me neither," said Teeny, cracking open a bag of potato chips in the backseat.

"Where did you get those chips ?" I asked.

"I keep a spare bag back here for longer trips."

"You store potato chips in my truck?" I asked.

"And in my convertible. And in May's van." Teeny

crunched down on a chip. "Sometimes I mix it up and get popcorn instead."

I laughed. Then the details of the case started elbowing out my amusement, and I got serious again. "For argument's sake, let's consider the possibility that Hannah lied. If she hated the open relationship all along, that means she had been angry with Buck for months or maybe even years. So if she killed Buck... why would she have waited and done it at the restaurant? Why wouldn't she have killed Buck months ago, at their home, where she could have more control over the crime scene?"

"Good point," said Miss May. "The location of the murder points to Petey. It's his restaurant. And he hated Buck. So Petey had motive and opportunity."

"But he seems innocent," said Teeny.

"Right." Miss May looked out the window and bit her thumbnail. "I'm just saying Petey remains a suspect, whether we like it or not. Maybe Rebecca figured out that Petey killed Buck. Maybe Rebecca confronted Petey so he had to kill her too."

"The missing link is this Jasmine girl," I said, following a road sign toward Brooklyn. "I bet she'll be able to tell us something we don't know."

Teeny nodded. "Or she's the killer and we need to prepare for a fight."

44

ALL SIGNS GREENPOINT TO YOU

*G*reenpoint was a charming combination of new and old. The community began as a refuge for Polish immigrants many, many years ago. A Polish stronghold remained. However, there had also been an influx of young professionals, some might say "hipsters," one of whom might have been Jasmine. As a result there were large luxury buildings scattered in with old brownstones, Polish restaurants, and cute little parks. The result was eclectic and pleasing.

Miss May, Teeny, and I gaped at the buildings and people as we crossed over into Greenpoint from neighboring Queens.

We soon found ourselves at the foot of *Twenty Five Locksley*. It was a luxurious new apartment building that stretched above the old brownstones. Although the building was four or five blocks in from the river, it looked to be at least twenty stories high, so I imagined most of the apartments had great water views. Most longtime New Yorkers despised buildings like 25 Locksley for displacing locals and

interrupting   otherwise   modest   neighborhoods   with
grandiosity.

Of course, I never liked the idea of people being forced
out of their own neighborhoods and the interior designer in
me recognized the value of the old architecture. But I always
loved those big, luxury buildings too. They were so shiny
and shimmering and, well, luxurious. I'd never lived in one
while I was a resident of the city, but a few of my friends had
and I'd enjoyed visiting their apartments, which were all
more spacious than mine and cleaner than mine and, most
importantly, did not contain any roaches.

Old buildings in the city almost always had roaches and
the hardy pests were challenging, to say the least.

Another nice thing about the luxury buildings? Great
security.

There was always a guard or two posted at the doors to
protect residents from unwanted visitors and solicitors. That
protection was no doubt a perk for residents. However, the
security team at 25 Locksley proved a challenge for a ragtag
group of amateur sleuths like me and the girls.

The doorman out front of the building had a security
patch on his jacket and a walkie-talkie on his hip. He was
big and burly and had a mustache that looked like it was
eating his face.

"How are we going to get past this guy?" said Teeny.
"Chelsea, you have any leftover feminine wiles?"

"I don't think feminine wiles are going to work on this
guy. He's all business."

"So we'll sneak in." Miss May looked the building up
and down. "Can't be that hard."

"You'd be surprised," I said. "After this security guard
there's going to be a desk inside with another. That second
security guard usually sits between the entrance and the

elevator so you need to pass them in order to access the rest of the building. Then sometimes you need a special key card just to make the elevator go up."

"These rich city people are ridiculous," said Teeny. "Like strangers are really so desperate to steal their stuff? This isn't Buckingham palace. It's just a nice, new building in Brooklyn. I used to come to this exact block when I was a girl to buy Kielbasa from a little old man with a dirty pushcart."

Miss May smiled. "I bet those were delicious."

"Oh, you have no idea. They would crack when you bit into them and then they were so juicy. I could go for one now. But no, poor dirty Kielbasa guy has been chased out by hipsters! And now I have to look up at this architectural monstrosity instead of eating a delicious brat? Look at this place. It looks like a vertical cruise ship. Do you think the residents get magic shows every night in the lobby?"

I shook my head. "They probably don't leave their apartments too often. Netflix is all the magic anyone wants these days."

"We need a plan," said Miss May. "If security is as robust as you say it is, I don't know how we're going to get in."

"I'll get in, no problem." Teeny brushed off her hands on her pants. "You just have to act like you own the place. Watch."

Teeny marched toward the front of the building with her chest puffed out and her head held high. She breezed right past the first security guard and disappeared into the lobby. A few seconds later, Teeny exploded back onto the sidewalk, yelling at the security guard inside. "You are a mean man. I'm going to report you and you're going to be fired! You hear me? You better call your mom, because you're moving back into the basement, loser."

Teeny charged back over to us. Both Miss May and I chuckled.

"How did that go?" asked Miss May.

"That guy is a jerk," said Teeny. "Also, I can never step inside that building again or he's going to have me arrested."

"What happened?" I asked.

"He wouldn't let me in the elevator unless I told him my name and gave him my license and told him who I was there to go see. That's an invasion of privacy."

"I told you security was serious," I said.

"Yeah but you didn't tell me they were going to need my fingerprints and Social Security number and a blood sample just to ride the elevator."

"Maybe we can sneak in through the parking area or something," said Miss May. "Is there parking underneath?"

I shook my head. "A building with parking is the Holy Grail of New York City living. There's no way inside this place except past those two security guards."

"OK," said Miss May. "So we need to regroup. We need a new plan."

"That's fine," said Teeny, "but first I need a Kielbasa. That guy's gotta be around here somewhere."

Teeny charged off, leading the way in search of her Polish sausage. Miss May and I followed.

Twenty minutes later, we had walked up and down every street in Greenpoint but we hadn't found a single Kielbasa. Teeny leaned on a railing looking out over the East River and groaned. "We passed fifteen fancy coffee shops but can't find one single Kielbasa? This neighborhood is turning into a dump."

"It's not that bad." I gestured to the sweeping views of the Manhattan skyline. "This view can't be beat."

"Whatever," said Teeny. "Just let me have my grief."

I looked around and spotted a long pier that jutted out into the river. Loud music played at the end of the pier and twenty or thirty people were crowded together there, dancing.

"Let's go down there," I said. "Maybe one of those random dancing people knows Jasmine."

Miss May looked over at me. "That's a stretch, Chelsea."

I shrugged. "Worth a shot. She lives a few blocks from here."

Miss May gave me a skeptical look. But I headed toward the pier and she and Teeny followed..

A few minutes later, the three of us stood at the edge of the throng of dancers. They all seemed to be having a great time, and many appeared to be having fun with the help of alcohol or some other illicit substance. The women rolled their arms through the air like jellyfish. The men twisted their hips with absent smiles on their faces. An effervescent young woman laughed as she twirled with her hands above her head.

"Hold on a second!" I pointed into the throng. "That's Jasmine. The twirling girl!"

Miss May put her hand to her forehead like a sailor gazing out to sea. "You're right. That's the girl from Rebecca's house. You need to get out there and talk to her, Chelsea."

I slouched my shoulders. "Why me?"

Miss May smirked. "Come on. We're too old to dance like that."

45

AGE IS JUST A NUMBER

"*N*o way. I'm not letting you get by with this old age excuse anymore. It's overused and it's discrimination against me for being young." I put my little foot down and looked at Teeny and Miss May with determination.

"It's not like we're making it up, Chelsea," said Teeny. "We're actually old."

"Oh you are not!" I said. "You're only old when it's a convenient excuse. The rest of the time you're all, 'age is just a number' and 'don't call me old!'"

Teeny chuckled. "Listen, Chelsea. Part of aging gracefully is knowing when to use your years to your advantage. Whether that means getting fun discounts or getting out of things you don't want to do. And neither of us want to go out into that pulsating mass of dancing weirdos and investigate. That's what you bring to the team."

"I respect you as my elders," I said. "But I also really, really, really don't want to go out there alone. Please don't make me do it. Please, please, please. I'm a terrible dancer. You both know about my sweat issues. If you make me do this... Well, I'll go, but I won't be happy and I will be sweaty."

Miss May looked out at the dancers at the end of the pier. She sighed. "OK." She held out her hand. I took it. "Let's show those kids what we've got."

I smiled. "Really? You'll dance with me?"

"Only to stop your annoying whining."

"I was not being annoying! I mean, I've let you two push me through windows and force me to give massages and all sorts of other things... Dancing is frankly the least offensive thing you've asked me to do. But sometimes a girl just can't take anymore."

Miss May chuckled. "It was the straw that broke the Chelsea's back, I suppose."

"Well I'm not going." Teeny crossed her arms. "I'm still miffed about my Kielbasa."

"That's fine," said Miss May. "You hang back here and observe."

Jasmine was at the very center of the circle of dancing people, protected by three rings of drunken twenty-some-things, all pulsing and gyrating in time with the music. Everyone in the circle danced like they were at a cool, underground club. Miss May and I, however, danced like we were at our uncle's wedding. We were stiff and weird and I was sure we looked like the kind of people who said things like, "I love to boogie."

"We need to get into the middle of that circle," I said.

"Let's dance our way in there," said Miss May. "I don't see any other options."

"How are we supposed to do that? Jasmine is dead center. Look at her. She's dancing like she got away with something. Too fluid. Too carefree."

"That's why we need to get in there and talk to her. I'll lead us into the middle. Ready?"

Before I had a chance to answer, Miss May lowered her shoulder and pulled me into the crowd with a ferocious swiftness. The dancers backed away, almost by instinct, and we entered the circle. I supposed that those Brooklyn people were caught off guard by a couple of upstate wedding guests like us.

Thirty seconds later, we were dancing right beside Jasmine. She was free and smooth, almost liquid. And Miss May and I moved like two cinderblocks that had come to life. I made eye contact with Jasmine and she gave me a little smile.

"You're a great dancer," I said.

Jasmine did a little twirl, pretending not to hear me. Then she edged out of the crowd and made a beeline toward a little cooler at the edge of the pier where I presumed the alcoholic beverages were kept cold.

"You scared her away," said Miss May. "Go after her!"

I knew there was no use arguing. There was no way Miss May was going to chase Jasmine down with me. I'd already dragged her onto the makeshift dance floor. My goodwill for the day had evaporated. So I accepted my duty and headed off toward the cooler.

As I gently shoved my way over to the cooler I decided that I needed to leave my old Chelsea personality behind me and become the kind of party girl to whom Jasmine would relate. I made a mental note not to talk about my sweaty armpits or apple orchards or tiny horses or my nerdy lion-obsessed boyfriend. I stood a little taller, unbuttoned the top two buttons of my shirt, and stuck a big, ecstatic smile on my face.

"This music is amazing," I said, digging in the cooler

next to Jasmine. I used a croaky, carefree voice like an exhausted sorority girl. It was the quintessential voice of the overworked, New York City party girl, grateful for a chance to unwind. "Dancing is like, life. A good song comes on and I just let myself move and forget all my stress, you know?"

"Tell me about it," replied Jasmine in an almost exact replica of my croaky voice. "I'm letting so many negative toxins out right now. We're all, like, so lucky that music exists in the world."

"Oh my goodness, I know," I said. "I had a death in my family this week. So I really needed to boogie!"

I said 'boogie.' Shoot! Lucky for me, Jasmine didn't notice.

"Oh my goodness, we're soul sisters," she said, wrapping me up in a hug. "I lost someone this week too. My lover was...murdered."

"Oh?" I said in a high-pitched squeal. This was a big revelation, and I struggled to maintain my composure. "That is tragic. What happened?"

"I have no idea. But the worst part is, I was so mad at him the day he died. I had just found out he had like, this other girlfriend. I mean, whatever, I'm not some sort of prude. We didn't have to like, be monogamous." She said *monogamous* like it was a dirty word. "But he was lying to me about it, which just isn't cool. I yelled at him so much. Then he was killed and I wished that I could've just had more time with him... Even though he was probably a jerk, deep down. Love is love, you know?"

"That's so crazy," I said. "Do you think... Do you think the other girlfriend found out about you and that she's the one who killed him?"

"I did think that, at first, but then she turned up dead too," said Jasmine. "Now I don't know what to think. You know, he...my boyfriend or whatever, he had been dealing with this ridiculous scandal at work. He was finally going to get away from that place and start a new life. A new life with me, actually. He told me that. Whatever. Maybe that was a lie too. All that's left to do now is dance. And drink."

Jasmine finally selected a beer from the cooler. Then she charged back into the middle of the circle, chugging her drink with wild abandon. I caught Miss May's eye from across the pier. I could tell my aunt wanted to know if I had gathered any useful information. And I was pretty sure I had.

46

PIERING INTO THE FUTURE

*W*e found Teeny at the other end of the pier, digging into a big, juicy Kielbasa. She had a smile on her face and a napkin tucked into her shirt like a bib.

"How did it go?" She asked with her mouth full of Kielbasa.

"Not as well as it did for you, I see," I said. "Where did you find that?"

"Some guy walked by pushing a cart. Not the same fella from my childhood. He's probably no longer with us. But I tell you, this is delicious! I would have bought one for each of you but I only had money for one."

Miss May laughed. "That's OK. I'm not in the mood for sausage anyway."

"Me neither," I said. "I still feel all jittery from my conversation with Jasmine."

Teeny lowered her Kielbasa. "So you did it. You made it to the center of the circle. You parted the Red Sea of hipsters."

"I guess you could say that," I said.

Teeny immediately launched into a series of what felt like several thousand questions. I answered the pertinent queries as best I could, then I summed up my entire conversation with Jasmine in a few quick sentences. As I retold the story of my conversation with our suspect at the cooler, I realized one detail stood out above all the others. "Jasmine referenced a scandal at *Peter's Land and Sea*," I said.

"Was she referring to the murder of the head chef?" asked Miss May.

I shook my head. "No. She said Buck had been dealing with a scandal at work and he was about to finally be free. Maybe that has something to do with his death."

"Maybe it has something to do with her relationship with Buck," said Miss May. "That whole open relationship thing sounds like it was pretty scandalous."

Teeny nodded. "Love triangles are always scandalous. Even in open relationships."

"Technically I think this was a love square," said Miss May. "At least."

"I don't know," I said. "Buck's many relationships doesn't seem like the thing Jasmine was referencing. It sounded like something separate from her relationship with Buck or his relationship with any women."

"Do you think there was something more going on at the restaurant that could have motivated these murders?" Miss May asked.

"I think it's possible there's an angle we haven't considered," I said. "Buck was a bad leader and a horrible boss. He left his job at *Hudgens* under unclear circumstances. And he'd already made a number of enemies at *Land and Sea*, including the owner. There's no telling who else at that place might have wanted Buck dead."

Teeny snapped her fingers. "I bet an angry, murderous

busboy snapped! He killed Buck because Buck was yelling too much. No. The busboy was in love with Rebecca. When the poor lovesick puppy found out that Rebecca and Buck had been romantic with one another, the kid snapped and killed Buck. Then he killed Rebecca because he knew he couldn't have her, even with Buck dead."

"Is that from *North Port Diaries*?" I asked.

Teeny shook her head. "That theory is all mine. Good, right? I've been waiting for an evil busboy to pop up in this town. Busboys are shady characters, the lot of 'em."

"That's a fine theory, Teeny," said Miss May. "But what about that new chef at *Hudgens*? Seems like he already knew Buck was dead and played dumb."

"That's true," I said. "We never really talked about that. As soon as we brought up Buck's death, that *Hudgen's* chef got weird. And how wouldn't he have found out about Buck's death? Everyone learns everything immediately these days on social media."

"Maybe Buck's big scandal started at *Hudgens* and followed him to Pine Grove," said Miss May. "If that's true, there could be a whole trove of suspects at *Hudgen's* we haven't considered yet."

"We're already down in the city," I said. "Should we pop back in to *Hudgens*?"

Miss May nodded. "I think we should, yes. But this time let's avoid the hostess and the chef. I want to go around the back, into the belly of the beast. Something tells me if we can talk to the servers and kitchen staff, they may be able to tell us everything we need to know."

47

ALLEY CATS

The three of us snuck down a dark alley toward the open back door of the *Hudgen's* kitchen on our tippy toes.

The sound of angry, heavy metal music blasted from inside the kitchen and sent a shock through my system. The pounding, heavy bass drum thumped in my temples. Squealing guitars raked across my brain. And guttural singing caused my fists to tighten. As we got closer to the restaurant, I felt as though my heart was beating in time with the music and my adrenaline pumped accordingly.

Miss May crouched behind a dumpster a safe distance from the kitchen door. Teeny and I crouched behind her.

"I love this music," said Teeny.

"You do?" I asked. "It's heavy metal. It doesn't seem like your vibe."

Teeny shrugged. "I'm surprised, too. But I think it suits my mood right now. I'm amped! I'm ready to go."

"Quiet down," said Miss May. "Someone's coming."

A muscular, bearded man emerged from the kitchen, opened the lid of the dumpster, and tossed in a hefty trash bag. When he cracked the lid of the dumpster, the fumes hit my nostrils and I coughed. The man must have heard me because seconds later, he was standing above us with his arms crossed like an angry prison guard.

"Who are you?" The man had a thick Russian accent to match what I quickly concluded was a thick Russian beard. "Get up."

The three of us got to our feet. Miss May pulled an apple pie from her purse. "Hi. Would you like—"

The big Russian snatched the pie, opened the container, reached in and grabbed a handful of the dessert like it was finger food. He shoved the pie in his mouth and the sides of his lips turned down in approval. "Not bad. You are here to sell desserts?"

"Actually, we were wondering if you might know a friend of ours..." Miss May gestured at me with her head and I pulled a picture of Buck up on my phone. I showed the photo to the muscular Russian.

"Ah! This man is so ugly. I hate his hideous face. He has beady little eyes and his beard is lackluster."

"Thank you," said Teeny. "I've always said he's ugly. He looks like a rat." She caught herself. "Nice guy, though. Mostly."

"No. You were right first time. He looks like ugly rat."

I put the phone back in my pocket. "So you don't recognize him?"

The Russian man turned, spat and looked back at me. "Lucky me I do not know the ugly man."

Miss May took a gentle step toward the Russian. "Do you think we could show this picture to some of the other kitchen employees?"

"Why?"

"Um... Um..." Miss May stammered.

"He's my long-lost brother," I said. "I did one of those genetic tests on the Internet and that's how I found him. Crazy, I know. After conducting more research I learned that my ugly missing brother worked, for a time, in the kitchen at this restaurant. You might not have expected that we're related because of his beady eyes and rat-like qualities and my comparably soft and sweet face... But make no mistake, that man is my brother. I want to know if anyone in your kitchen has seen him. Please. He's my only family."

The Russian crossed his arms and looked me up and down. The weight of my ridiculous lie was heavy on my shoulders but I tried to stand up straight and look innocent and hopeful. It must have worked because the Russian invited us in with a grunt and a wave.

Miss May accepted the Russian's invitation into the kitchen but I grabbed her arm and stopped her before we entered. "We can't just walk in there. Jeffrey is going to recognize us."

Miss May peeked inside the kitchen. "We'll stay back near the dishwasher. Jeffrey won't have any reason to visit that area. I think we'll be able to fly under the radar."

I took a deep breath. "OK."

Seconds later, we were huddled behind an enormous, industrial dishwasher along with five nearly identical Eastern European men. The Russian explained my predicament about the long-lost brother to his co-workers, or at least that's what I think he was saying, because he motioned for me to pull up the picture on my phone.

I opened to the picture of Buck and handed it to the Russian, who then allowed the other men to pass the phone among themselves. One by one, each man looked at the photo, muttered something in Russian, shrugged and passed the photo on. Finally, the Russian returned the phone to my possession. "They do not know your ugly brother. My apologies."

"They have to know him," said Teeny. "He worked here for a long time. If they don't know his face, maybe they know his name." Teeny took a big step toward the group of dishwashers and spoke at her maximum volume. "Buck Johnson. Buck. Johnson."

The men grumbled in Russian and shrugged, once more one after another, like they were doing the wave at Yankee Stadium with only their shoulders.

The big bearded Russian stepped between Teeny and the other employees. "They do not know of the ugly brother. I already said." The Russian's eyes tightened as his nostrils flared. "Now stop harassing us. We are busy at work."

Teeny repeated Buck's name once more, as loud as she possibly could, as though the volume of her voice would somehow change the truth of the situation. But she was a little too loud, because the sound of her voice lured Jeffrey toward us from deeper in the kitchen.

"Hey!" Jeffrey said, pointing a finger at us. "What are you doing here? Stop badgering my staff."

Miss May widened her eyes. "Oh! Hello. Sorry. We just loved our meal here the other day so much we dropped by to thank these men for their hard work."

The Russian scrunched up his nose. "What about ugly brother?"

I grabbed Teeny and Miss May by the wrists and pulled them out of the kitchen. "OK. Bye. Thanks for everything!"

We emerged from the alley back onto a busy New York Avenue and I let out a deep exhale. "Oh my goodness, that was close. Teeny. You were yelling so loud. I didn't know you could reach that decibel."

Teeny shrugged. "I was inspired by that metal stuff. Those guys can really scream."

"You did a great job," said Miss May. "We got some important information in there."

"How is that?" I asked. "None of those guys recognized Buck in the slightest."

Miss May waved my concern away. "Kitchen staff changes all the time. It's entirely possible those guys never met Buck. But did you see the way Jeffrey reacted when he saw us? When he heard Teeny screaming Buck's name? He freaked out. There must be something more to this restaurant and Buck's position there than what we've learned so far."

"What we do now ?" I asked. "It's not like we can go back and have another meal now. The guy hates us."

"We're going to have a good, old-fashioned stakeout," said Miss May. "Right behind our favorite dumpster."

Miss May skulked back toward the dumpster adjacent to the *Hudgens* rear entrance. Teeny and I had no choice but to follow, so we did. Then the three of us sat with our backs against the cold metal of the dumpster and waited.

For the longest time, nothing notable happened. The bearded Russian took out a few more bags of trash. A couple of the other Russian guys leaned against the back door and smoked cigarettes while muttering in their surly native tongue. A server stepped out back to engage in an angry phone call with her boyfriend and called him a few choice names.

Then someone zipped through the alley on a messenger bike and hopped off behind *Hudgens*. It was a man in his thirties wearing tight, cuffed jeans and a leather jacket.

The man lurked in the shadows, pulled out his phone and fired off a text. A few seconds later, a busboy emerged from the restaurant holding a brown paper bag. The busboy looked both ways to make sure that he was alone in the alley. Then the bicycle messenger emerged from the shadows and met the busboy right beside the dumpster.

"You got the stuff?" asked the bike messenger.

"Two pounds. Just like you asked. But remember... You didn't get it from me."

The bike messenger handed the busboy a generic paper bag, then the busboy disappeared inside and bike messenger road away.

"What was that?" I said.

"I don't know," said Miss May. "But we better catch that bike."

I nodded, sprung to my feet, and started after the bike messenger. He turned onto the street and I lagged at least fifty feet behind him. But then the bicyclist got caught at a red light. I reached him just as the light turned green again. He began to pedal but I jumped out and tackled him side-ways. It was not my most graceful move, but it was effective. We both crashed to the ground with a thud and the paper bag the bike messenger had gotten from *Hudgen's* tumbled onto the sidewalk.

"Whoa! You're crazy, lady! What are you doing?"

"I'm solving a murder, I think," I said. "What did you just buy from *Hudgens Restaurant*?"

"Baseball cards, dude! Relax. The busboy put an ad online. He said I had to meet him at work."

"Baseball cards. Oh. Really?"

"Really!"

The bike messenger grabbed the brown paper bag, shoved it into his backpack, and pedaled away. I watched him go, confused. Then Miss May and Teeny arrived at my side and I told them all about my altercation.

When I finished, Miss May shook her head, skeptical. "I don't think that guy bought baseball cards from *Hudgens*," she said.

"Why not?" I asked.

Miss May squatted down and gathered a few items from the roadside. "Because these are high end truffles. And I don't think truffles grow in the streets of New York."

48

THE TROUBLE WITH TRUFFLES

*T*eeny snatched a truffle from Miss May's hand, brought it to her nose and sniffed. The sides of her mouth turned down and she looked away, trying to stifle a gag.

"There's something wrong with these truffles," Teeny said, choking out the words. "They smell horrible. And not just because they're truffles. There's something off. Why would that guy have paid for these?"

Miss May shrugged. "Can I smell?"

Teeny recoiled. "You don't want to smell these. If you've ever trusted me in your life, trust me now. It's horrible. Putrid."

"I'll be fine," Miss May insisted.

"OK," Teeny said. "Don't say I didn't warn you as hard as I could."

Teeny held out a palm full of truffles to Miss May. Miss May leaned in and smelled. It was a long, deep whiff. I cringed. Then, Miss May turned away and coughed for a long moment.

Teeny shook her head. "Told you so."

Miss May wiped tears away from her reddened eyes. "That's horrible. Chelsea, you have to smell."

"No way."

"Come on," said Miss May. "You can't be the only one who wouldn't smell it."

"You're acting like a third-grade boy," I said. "I don't want to smell the nasty thing. Thank you very much. I want to figure out who killed our victims and why."

Miss May stepped out of the street and onto the sidewalk just as an angry cabdriver yelled expletives in her direction.

"You have a nice day, too," said Miss May. "Things like that really make me miss the city. Such character. Such passion, everywhere you look. We should come down more."

"I don't know if I could handle running into that kind of passion every single day," said Teeny. "I have a bit too much passion of my own."

A few angry pedestrians pushed their way past us, then Miss May led us over to a vestibule where we could talk relatively unmolested.

"OK," I said, once we were safely nestled in the vestibule, "who has a theory?"

Miss May held up her hand like a kid in school. "I do."

"Share," I said.

"Buck got hired to turn things around at *Peter's Land and Sea*. At first, Buck thought his *Culinary Institute of America*-approved cooking skills would bring in more diners. But he was wrong. He knew he needed something flashy and unique to convince the people of Pine Grove to give him a shot, and to attract diners from the city and the rest of the Hudson Valley region."

"Oh my goodness," I said, realizing where Miss May might be headed. "So you think—"

Miss May nodded. "Buck was buying expired truffles, meats and other ingredients from *Hudgens* at a discount and then serving them at *Peter's Land and Sea*. He figured us country folk would be too stupid to tell the difference between quality ingredients and trash. And at first, it worked. All those fancy ingredients packed the restaurant. But things got more complicated when the patrons of *Land and Sea* began getting sick from Buck's food."

"And you think Buck did all this behind Petey's back?"

Miss May exhaled. "He was the kind of man who didn't like taking orders from a young restauranteur, you over-heard as much when you were hiding in the dumpster that day. I would bet anything that Buck demanded total control of sourcing ingredients and budgeting at the restaurant, so I suspect Petey didn't know a thing."

"I don't know," said Teeny. "Something about that theory doesn't add up. Buck is this renowned, fancy chef. He was a star pupil at the *Culinary Institute*, remember? Why would someone like that feed their customers rotten food? Seems to me like that kind of thing goes against everything Buck would have believed in."

Miss May looked up with a start. "Maybe it was against Buck's ethics, but what about Hannah's? Chelsea, you said there were ingredients lists and prices on her computer in the back office?"

"Yeah," I said, "but it seemed liked the office was shared by Hannah and Petey."

"But suppose I was wrong about Buck maintaining control over the inventory and purchasing," said Miss May. "Petey might have maintained control over that part of the process. Or maybe he delegated to Buck and then Buck delegated to Hannah. Either way, whoever sourced the foul ingredients didn't tell Buck what they were up to. My suspicion is that they mixed good truffles in with bad truffles, for instance, so Buck wouldn't notice. Or maybe they just gambled that the second-rate ingredients would still be edible. That way the restaurant saved money on top shelf product and the angry head chef never needed to know."

"That's so short sighted," I said. "Who would ever think rotten ingredients could help a restaurant succeed in the long run?"

"Maybe a new restaurateur?" said Miss May. "I hate to say it. But Petey is suddenly our prime suspect."

"You're right," said Teeny. "Hannah had no financial interest in *Land and Sea*. So she had no motive to save the restaurant money. But Petey had plenty of motivation to try to save some cash. I can see it now. Buck found out about the rotten ingredients, so he quit and threatened to report Petey. Petey couldn't allow that. The fate of his restaurant rested on its reputation. So he tried to kill Buck in a way that might seem innocent... Through a cinnamon bun. Petey didn't realize a poisoned cinnamon bun and a dead chef might also damage his reputation. Ever since then he's been a sneaky little mongoose, lying to our faces, scurrying around, and trying to cover up his evil crime." Teeny looked up with a big pout planted on her lips. "I raised a killer."

Miss May gave Teeny a hug and sighed. "We don't know that Petey is the killer, Teeny. And you didn't raise him. He worked at your restaurant for a few months."

Teeny pulled away from the hug. "You're right. This isn't my fault. I should stop being so hard on myself."

Miss May and I chuckled. Then we walked back to the car and sped back to Pine Grove with the destination of *Peter's Land and Sea* in the GPS. We called the restaurant a few times on our way up, but no one answered the phone. *Weird, considering we were in the heart of the Sunday afternoon rush.* Teeny tried Petey's personal phone but didn't get an answer there, either.

I glanced at the speedometer. I was already going well over the speed limit, but I pushed a little harder. We needed to get home fast because it seemed our killer, or killers, might have already been on the run.

49

MISSING PERSONS

*P*eter's *Land and Sea* was dark, quiet, and locked. Hannah's home was much the same. That meant there was only one place left to check for our suspected murderers...

....Petey's little apartment near town hall.

Teeny gasped as I pulled my pickup into a middle spot between a pair of beat up sedans. "That's Hannah's car. And that one is Petey's! They're both here. I knew it. They were in on these murders together! Petey held the gun and Hannah pulled the trigger."

"That's a serious partnership," I said. "I've never heard of a gun that needed two people to be operated."

"You know what I mean, Chelsea," said Teeny. "It's a metaphor or a simile or whatever. Is now really the time for you to pick apart my language?"

"Sorry." I looked up at Petey's apartment. "You're right. We have way more important things to do."

"And every second we spend talking is a second wasted," said Miss May, climbing out of the truck. "Let's go."

Miss May headed up the stairs toward Petey's apartment

with me and Teeny hot on the heels of her muddy work boots. She knocked on the door but no one answered. Then she tried to peer through the side window but the blinds were drawn. We couldn't see anything.

"We need to get in there," said Miss May, her voice in a low whisper. "But how?"

"We could throw this brick through the window." Teeny held out a brick. "I found it in the parking lot and thought it might come in handy."

Teeny pulled the brick back and readied a throw. Miss May stepped in the way to stop her. "No bricks! Too loud. Too aggressive. But I appreciate your forward thinking."

"I'll keep the brick on me just in case," said Teeny, mirroring Miss May's whisper.

I tried the front door. It was unlocked. "You guys. Look."

Miss May sighed and shook her head in frustration. "Alright. Stay quiet in there. And stay alert. It might be dangerous."

"Should I go first?" I asked.

Miss May nodded. Teeny offered up the brick. "Want the brick? Just in case?"

I took the brick and shouldered the door open and stepped into Petey's apartment. Dust hung suspended in a beam of sunlight. Other than that the place was dark. And it was quieter than a synagogue on Christmas.

I looked back at Miss May for instruction. She held her finger to her lips and pointed down a narrow hallway that led to an ancillary room. Probably the bedroom.

I pressed my back against the wall and sidestepped toward the room at the end of the hall. Miss May and Teeny did the same. The three of us must have looked like the world's most unlikely members of SEAL Team Six.

There was a loud thud from inside the room. We

stopped about halfway down the hall and listened. All was quiet. I took another sideways step toward the room. Then another. My adrenaline surged. I could feel my heart beating in my neck. And I felt as though I'd just chugged a quadruple espresso.

I reached out for the handle to the bedroom door but before I touched it the door swung open. There stood Hannah, holding a glistening butcher knife, sweaty and bedraggled.

"Get out of this apartment." Hannah thrust the knife in our direction. "Leave. Now."

"Don't hurt them," a voice gargled from behind Hannah. I looked. Petey was tied up in an office chair, writhing around in an attempt to get free.

"Shut up, Petey." Hannah did not look away from me, Teeny, and Miss May.

"Why are you doing this to me?" said Petey. "I thought you loved me. We had that magical night, with the flowers and the wine—"

"Stop making me repeat myself," said Hannah. "I was in an open relationship. You weren't special. You were one of many meaningless flings."

Teeny scratched her head. "Hold on a second. You and Petey were... involved?"

"And now she's trying to kill me!" Petey exclaimed.

"But she doesn't want to kill you over all these love affairs, does she?" asked Miss May. "She wants to kill you because—"

"Alright, I guess if you're not gonna leave, we're gonna have to do this the hard way. Get in the bedroom, old lady," Hannah snarled. "All three of you get inside and stand facing the wall. Hands up. And Chelsea, drop that brick."

I dropped the brick and winced at the loud thud it made on the wood floor.

"OK. Now get inside before I stab you all. To death," Hannah said.

"You don't kill people with knives, Hannah. You kill them with poison. Cyanide in a cinnamon bun, to be exact. That blade you're holding now is just for show." Miss May pulled out her phone. "I think I'll call the police instead."

My eyes widened. Miss May had an impressive poker face under threat of stabbing. I liked it.

But Hannah turned on her heels and threw the knife toward Petey. The blade just missed Petey's shoulder and stuck in the wall behind him. When Hannah turned back she was holding a handgun and pointing it right at Miss May's head. "Get in."

We marched into the bedroom in a single-file line.

"Face the wall behind Petey. Hands up. No turning around."

We did as we were told. But Miss May was in a sassy mood that day. "What's your plan here, Hannah? You're going to execute us and Petey and then make a run for it?"

Hannah pulled the knife from the wall, all the while keeping her gun trained on us. "Shut up. I'm thinking."

"You're never going to get away with this," said Teeny.

"Quiet!" said Hannah. "And drop that brick!"

Teeny dropped a second brick with a pout. "There goes my secret weapon."

"You had another brick?!" I whispered to Teeny.

She shrugged. "There was a whole pile of 'em out there."

"Do you really want to kill four more people just to maybe get away with a little bit of money?" Miss May asked Hannah.

"Be quiet so I can think!" said Hannah.

"Maybe I can think for you," said Miss May. "Help you reason this out. Your problems all started back when Buck worked at *Hudgens*, right? You didn't work there with him. But he would come home at night and complain about a scam that the owner, Jeffrey, was running. Selling expired ingredients in the alley behind the restaurant. Lining his pockets. I bet Buck tried to get Jeffrey to stop the scam. But Jeffrey refused. So Buck quit and sought refuge in Pine Grove, where he figured he could find a restaurant and run the kitchen however he pleased. The naïve young owner even let Buck hire you, Buck's wife, as the hostess. So sweet."

I craned my neck around so I could get a better look at the scene unfolding in the bedroom. Hannah's eyes were wide.

"But when you started working at *Land and Sea*, you saw the restaurant was struggling. You knew Petey was in over his head, and Buck was letting his arrogance get in the way of his business sense. Plus, Petey and Buck were so dysfunctional as a team that they were piling extra jobs on you. Making you work too hard. So you saw an opportunity to make a little extra cash. And you took it. You used Petey's money to buy ingredients from *Hudgens*. Truffles, meats, cheeses, whatever. You told Petey the stuff was top-of-the line, very expensive. Meanwhile, you were buying trash from *Hudgens* at a steep discount and pocketing the difference. You didn't have any problems ruining the reputation of *Peter's Land and Sea* by serving expired food because you felt unappreciated there. You wanted to make quick money, maybe to fund a life away from Buck, and you didn't care what happened to the restaurant in the long term. Then all the stupid locals started getting sick. Not every customer. But enough of them. You tried to keep the unhappy customers quiet so you could keep your racket running a little longer. You paid off most of the customers to shut their traps. People like Ethel, who needed the extra cash to fund her poker games. *Peter's* catering at *Washington Villages* made poor little old Ethel violently ill. But you bought her silence. I bet that's how Brian finally afforded to fix his espresso machine, too. He ate at *Land and Sea* and got sick, so you paid him off. These people, and others like them, thought you were being generous and apologetic. They had no idea you were bribing them to keep quiet so you could keep poisoning people with rancid food. But you couldn't keep the scam going forever, could you? Eventually, Buck figured the whole thing out. And that's when the problems really started."

The gun trembled in Hannah's hand. "Buck was a coward. And a hypocrite. He wasn't mad that people got sick. He was mad about how it would make him look."

"I bet Buck told Petey about your scam, didn't he?" said Miss May. "But Petey loved you, after your torrid one night stand. He refused to believe you were capable of hurting him or anyone else. Buck and Petey argued about it but Petey couldn't see the truth. Petey refused to fire you. So Buck quit. And he made a plan to tell the cops all about your rotten ingredient hustle."

Hannah stammered. Miss May continued. "So you killed your husband. Then Rebecca revealed that she knew about what you did to Buck — she probably saw you baking the cinnamon bun that poisoned her lover — so you killed her, too. Eventually Petey figured the whole thing out. Realized Buck had been telling the truth. And that's probably why he's tied up behind you. Although I still don't think you're willing to shoot any of us in cold blood, so you might as well put the gun down and turn yourself in."

"Wow," said Petey. "Miss May, that was amazing. If my hands weren't tied up I would totally clap."

"Shut up, Petey!" Hannah snapped. "You have no idea what you're talking about, May. Rebecca... Rebecca didn't even care that Buck was dead! You know what she cared about? Herself! Saving her own skin."

"Ah, of course. Because you put Rebecca in danger to protect yourself...after Rebecca figured out you had framed her for Buck's murder." Miss May spoke in a relaxed tone. "The cyanide in the cinnamon could be traced to her tincture workshop, right? Because of the cassava in one of her potions. You wanted us to think Rebecca committed this crime, but your plan didn't work. In fact, Rebecca was going to expose you. So you took care of the problem."

"I'm not a crazy villainess," said Hannah. "I'm not even a criminal! I needed to be able to take care of myself once Buck and I were divorced. That wasn't gonna happen on what Petey was paying me. I barely made more than minimum wage!"

"Listen—" Miss May took a step toward Hannah.

Bang! Bang!

Hannah fired two shots into the ceiling. Miss May, Teeny, and I dropped to our knees and covered our heads, screaming. We stayed curled up and frozen for a few seconds. Then a door slammed in the distance.

I turned back and Hannah was gone.

I leapt to my feet and darted out of the apartment. By the time I got out to the parking lot, Hannah was already in her car, driving away. So I jumped into my truck, swung around to pick up Teeny and Miss May — waited for them to descend the stairs — and squealed out of the parking lot in pursuit of the cold-blooded killer.

50

RACE TO THE FINISH

*P*ine Grove's Fall Fest was in full swing that Sunday afternoon, with happy kids, vendors and performers abound. Everyone looked happy and peaceful. Until, that is, Hannah drove head-on into a police barrier, jumped out of her car and took off running through the crowds.

I slammed on my brakes right behind Hannah's car and jumped out, darting after her with all the vigor my little legs could manage.

If I hadn't been in the middle of chasing down a confessed murderer, I might have stopped to appreciate the charm of the festival. Little girls were getting their faces painted like pumpkins. Mayor Linda Delgado was dressed up like a scarecrow. And an elderly woman struggled to get her dentures unstuck from a bright red candy apple.

I did a spin move around the toothless old woman and narrowly avoided crashing into a table that had been set up for a pumpkin carving contest.

Twenty feet ahead of me, Hannah leapt over a bale of

hay. Then she turned back, picked it up and threw it in my direction to create an obstacle.

It worked.

The bale of hay hit me square in the chest and I stumbled back a few feet. But I recovered quickly and closed the gap between me and Hannah right as she approached a massive cornucopia display.

I was five feet away from Hannah when Brian from the *Brown Cow* pushed his coffee cart right into my path. I scrambled to get around the cart but Hannah used the opportunity to increase the distance between us. "Catch that woman," I said. "Stop her!"

I took a deep breath and resumed running as fast as I could, which was unfortunately not that fast. Yeah, I was proficient at karate, and yeah, sometimes I had to chase people, but I needed more cardio in my workout regimen. Who am I kidding? I needed a workout regimen. And some new deodorant. Because that chase got me sweaty.

Luckily, the people of Pine Grove heeded my call and joined me in the chase for Hannah. At first, it was just a couple of kids running by my side. But when I looked back, a large throng of townspeople had joined me in my pursuit. And Detective Wayne Hudson was just inches behind me.

"Hannah's the killer?" he called up to me.

"Yes," I panted. "And she's getting away."

"I suspected her," Wayne said, "but wasn't sure about her motive. They were in an open relationship. You know that, right?"

"Can we talk about this later?" I asked, gasping for breath.

Up ahead, Hannah pushed a little girl off a bicycle, stole the bike and pedaled away. Hannah made a hard right turn at Pine Grove's only stoplight. I followed, as did the herd of townspeople. When I turned the corner I saw that a giant banner had been stretched across the street and it read: "Will you marry me, Chelsea?"

My eyes widened. *I had forgotten all about Germany.*

My mind raced almost as fast as my feet. I remembered Germany declaring there would be a surprise at the Fall Festival. And I also remembered that he had called my phone a dozen times over the course of that day. *Probably to confirm I would be attending the Festival...*

I felt bad but also a little confused. *Is that where Germany and I were in our relationship? Marriage? He lived in Africa! And did I really want to be proposed to via a giant banner in front of everyone in town?*

Hannah saw the banner too late. She rode the bike right into it and fell backwards with a startled shriek. As Hannah scrambled to untangle herself from my marriage proposal, Wayne and I caught up to her.

Hannah snarled when she saw me. "Stay away from me." She climbed to her feet and attacked, smacking and clawing at me like a wild animal. I reeled for an instant, holding my hands up in a defensive posture. But then I remembered I could fight back.

With one quick kick to the knees, I dropped Hannah to the ground. The second Hannah went down, Wayne handcuffed and Mirandized her. Germany's banner ripped in half as Wayne dragged Hannah off the street and into a nearby squad car.

When I turned back to the crowd, the whole town exploded with applause. Brian from the *Brown Cow* called out an apology. Petunia and Ethel flashed me a thumbs up. The toothless apple eater gave me a big, gummy grin. And Miss May and Teeny pushed their way to the front and wrapped their arms around me.

"We tried to keep up but we're too old," said Miss May.

I laughed. "I thought I told you to stop using that excuse."

The crowd parted to make way as Germany Turtle walked toward me with a bouquet of at least a hundred roses. It was so big, it blocked his face from view. He laid the bouquet in my arms and dropped to one knee.

Oh boy.

"Chelsea," he said. "Your beauty shines, as if the sun, the moon, and the stars were all concentrated into one single, magnificent light. Your intellect sparkles, as if all of the world's great thinkers throughout history joined together in one brain more brilliant than each of them combined. Your eyes glitter with a deep, infinite clarity, like the pool at the bottom of Niagara Falls. When I met you, I was an orphan. A sad, broken man child. But you put me back together again and showed me how to be a man. You accepted my love of mismatched denim and you supported my mission with the lions in Africa. Your bravery inspires me anew with each passing day and your karate skills continue to surprise and impress me. Nothing would make me happier, my sweet Chelsea Thomas, than for you to become my wife. What do you say? Will you marry me?"

All of the voices and sounds and images around me dropped away, and suddenly all I saw was Germany's sweet, guileless face before me. The world seemed to move in slow-motion. A monarch butterfly glided past my field of vision, and I felt like I could see entire lifetimes between each flap of its wings.

I wanted to say yes. And I could tell the crowd wanted that too.

But did I want to spend my life with Germany Turtle?

"Germany. I love you," I said. "That was beautiful and you're incredible. But I need time. I have to think about it."

The entire crowd exhaled simultaneously and I felt like I had just missed the winning buzzer beater at a championship basketball game.

Germany stood, mumbled a few unintelligible words and hurried away. Silent tears streamed down my cheeks as I watched Germany disappear into the Fall Fest crowd.

"Are you OK?" Wayne asked from nearby.

I shook my head. I had no idea.

51

A MODEST PROPOSAL

*T*he next day we had a huge party at the orchard to celebrate another case closed. Miss May baked up a few big pans of her big, gooey apple pie cookies, aka Appie Oaters. I was in charge of the hot apple cider station. And Tom Gigley's band, *The Giggles*, played a set list of pure Frank Sinatra covers, but with a rock n' roll edge. It was an odd choice but everyone knew all the words, which was fun.

You know those days when the air is the exact right temperature, so that it's not cold in the shade but the sun still feels like a welcome heat whenever the breeze stops blowing? That was the kind of day we had. And I wanted to enjoy it. But I couldn't get my head out of the turtle-shaped clouds.

The prior night I had barely slept, tossing and turning and thrashing and sweating because I felt so bad for the way I had handled Germany's proposal.

I hadn't given enough thought to Germany's promised surprise prior to the Fall Festival. If I'd considered it for even one minute, I could have anticipated what was coming and prevented Germany from embarrassing himself by proposing in such a bold and public way. We could have talked in private and we both would have felt so much better. But as it stood Germany was humiliated, which was incredibly rare for him. He had a high tolerance for shame, but I'd hurt him. I felt guilty and confused and, like I said, distracted.

Petey approached my apple cider table with a little wave. "Hi, Chelsea."

"Hey, Petey. You came to the party. Even though we hard-core suspected you of murder."

"I know how it is," Petey said. "You suspected me because you had plenty of good reasons. I'm not going to hold that against you. Pine Grove is lucky to have all three of you. Can I get some of that cider?"

I poured Petey an apple cider and handed him the cup. He sipped it. "Mmmm. This is so smooth. It warms my whole body."

"I know, it is delicious," I said. "I drink way too much of it, though. I guess that's part of life when you live on an orchard. Apple cider flows like water around here."

Petey laughed, then got serious. "Hey, so have you heard the news?"

"So much has happened in the last day, I'm not sure which news you mean."

"I guess it's kind of personal news for me. I'm closing down *Peter's Land and Sea*. Yeah. Bummer. But Teeny hired me on as the manager over at *Grandma's*. She's gone so much these days, working cases with you and your aunt, she needs the extra help. I think it's going to be nice. And it's definitely going to be less stressful for me. I was losing a ton of money on the restaurant."

"That sounds great," I said. "I think Teeny always secretly wanted you back."

Petey wandered away, sipping his apple cider. And I did my best to stay present and keep my mind from drifting back to my feelings.

Then I heard barking from across the party. It sounded like Steve the dog. And he didn't sound happy. I left my post at the apple cider station and hurried toward the sound of the barks.

I soon found Steve in the arms of Amy, the dog groomer. She spoke in a gentle voice but Steve kept barking. "Hey, buddy. It's OK. Look. Chelsea's here. See? Chelsea?"

I looked Steve in the eye. "What's going on, Steve? Why are you freaking out?"

Steve barked a few more times, then broke free from Amy and trotted out toward the orchard. He stopped at the edge of the trees and turned back to me with an expectant look.

"Maybe he has to go to the bathroom?" said Amy.

"Maybe," I replied. But I knew something more was going on with Steve and I feared the worst.

Once we were about a hundred feet out into the orchard, Steve started digging. My mind flashed back to the end of our prior mystery. That time, Steve had unearthed a human foot for me. *Some congratulations gift, right?*

"Relax, Steve," I said. "Everything's OK. Go ahead. Show me what's in your hole."

Steve stepped aside. I squatted and looked into the hole. My stomach turned. There, unmistakably identifiable in the dirt, was a disembodied human hand, clearly severed from the same body as the unidentifiable feet.

There were three big, chunky rings on the fingers. And that's how I knew whose hand it was.

Deep down, I prayed the man was alive. But deeper still, I knew he was dead. The man had been famous in Pine

Grove. Or infamous, depending who you asked. And no one had even reported him missing.

So how had this local legend ended up in pieces scattered around our orchard?

I wasn't sure of the answer, but I was sure of one thing... It was time to solve another mystery in Pine Grove.

The End

Dear Reader,

Thank you for reading *The Smoking Bun*. I hope you enjoyed this mystery and that you had a good time following the twists and turns along with the girls.

Adventure awaits you in the next apple orchard cozy, *Dropping Like Pies*.

You'll love this cozy because everyone loves exciting mysteries with quirky amateur detectives.

Search *Dropping Like Pies* on Amazon.

Grab your copy today.

Best,
Chelsea

P.S. Amy the Dog Groomer now has her own cozy mystery series. You'll love this series because everyone loves mysteries with cute tiny animals! Search "Dog Groomer Mysteries" on Amazon to order Book One today!

Made in United States
Troutdale, OR
08/29/2023

12462857R00159